The Mecrutian Chronicles

Heart of Shell

ZARA STEEN

UNICORN

ISBN 13: 978-0-9917830-4-5
ISBN 10: 0991783042

THE MERCRUTIAN CHRONICLES: HEART OF SHELL

Copyright by Smarin Publishing © May 2015. All rights reserved. Printed through Amazon CreateSpace. Edited by Annette Malchow. No part of this book may be used or reproduced in any manner whatsoever without written permission of the publisher, except in the case of brief quotations expressed in critical articles and reviews. For information address Smarin Publishing: stephaniemarin@gmail.com.

This is a work of fiction. Names, characters, places and incidents are either the product of the authors imagination and creativity or are used fictitiously. Any resemblance to persons, alive or dead, businesses, events or communities is entirely coincidental.

For my parents

thank you for instilling
the confidence to dream.

Lilli,
Uncover
your world of
magic and
unlock your
inner mermaid
xo

Acknowledgments

I'm blessed to have readers like you who have taken a moment to visit my world and meet my characters. For you, I'm thankful. I hope you'll stay a while and enjoy.

This book never would have been completed without the encouragement and support of my partner, Jeff Neumann. Thank you for still loving me despite my long hermit-like writing sessions and my incessant book brained attitude.

Annette Malchow, thank you so much for being such an amazing person in my life who is supportive of my writing The book has matured to a new level thanks to you. I appreciate you reviewing the things that just didn't jive. You're a great editor.

National Novel Writing Month was also instrumental in encouraging me to carve out the time to put these words to page. That amazing program, and fun opportunity is something I encourage all writers to explore, please see more about it at: www.nanowrimo.org

Chapter 1

TONIGHT WAS COLDER than the deep of the ocean. I hadn't been there for a long time, but I remembered the way it felt. The smoothness of the water there was silky, icy, and truly pure. It was calming to me, purifying for the soul.

It was midnight blue outside the car, the trees blending as we moved, blurring like the depths of my father's birthplace. He was named, Kanja, meaning 'water born' because he was water born, just like me. It seemed peculiar that my mother was born ashore since she was the only full Mer among the three of us.

The sky outside crackled with lightning in the distance, and were it not for the fact that we had left behind another dismal failure I would take it as a warning sign for us to turn back. A roar of thunder broke against the splashing sound of water sloshing beneath the car's tires; yet the storm ahead was softened by the rain, and the downpour was soothing, pattering softly on the window and rippling down in errant spirals.

My mother looked back at me while my father drove. Her long auburn hair was shimmering in the flickers of light passing through the window from the oncoming highway traffic. Looking at her I admired her flawless, pearlescent skin. Her hazel eyes were flecked with bits of blue and teal like a true Mer. My mother was beautiful, and I looked nothing like her.

"Anya," she said to me reaching back to clasp a hand in mine, her cream hand tracing over my toffee coloured fingers. "Are you well?"

"Fine Mother," I replied softly, still watching the rain and wishing that I could open the window and stick my hand out.

Our destination was not much farther, an hour at most, but the travelling was tiresome. I should be used to it by now; we had moved all over the continent of North America in the past four years, making our way from outpost to outpost for my parent's scientific research. Or at least until I had turned twelve and they began a relentless search for my mate. Then, that had meant even more travel, more nights and days spent on the road searching in the name of custom.

In the dark of the night, I could see everything in the car. Despite needing to wear braces, my eyes were perfect, just like any other Mer. The opened journal on my lap was blank, waiting to be marked with words. I grabbed a pen from my bag and I almost began to write 'Dear Diary', but pulled my hand back before the black ink scratched the surface. That saying felt too cliché, too human. Even 'Dear Journal' -a seemingly more mature version- didn't quite work for me. Instead I opted for my name, Anya. I figured this could be a letter so that later, when I was an old and decrepit siren lying at the bottom of the sea I could look back and remember it all. I stopped writing before I'd begun. Instead I remembered what I had left behind; a few friends who though not close, might have been decent enough to celebrate my birthday with me.

"Good luck, Tiger Shark," Maya had said with a wink, "thirteen was a bad year, but thankfully your last year of grade school is over, and fourteen can be a fresh start." She was older than me, already fifteen and mated to a Mer one outpost over. Her gifts were in full blossom, her beauty growing daily, while I felt I had accomplished nothing. She had always been kind to me though, and I knew we would stay in touch.

At least in leaving the past, I could leave behind the memory of Shoal, the blue eyed Mer-god who turned me down like all the others. Sometimes I hated being mostly Mer. We weren't meant to be on land, science or no science. Soaking in a bathtub was nothing compared to being out there in the deep. I only tolerated land life more because of being a quarter human, and it's only ever made more problems for me. My humanity has stopped me from my full potential. Even my father, being half human hadn't experienced such problems with his transcendence.

"Almost there Anya," my father said, breaking my thoughts. He glanced over to my mother. His dark brown eyes glimmered in the night, the irises circled by a ring of blue. His caramel skin was darker than mine, but my locks were the same rich brown. Only *his* hair was enchanted by the sea and woven with essence.

"Okay Dad," I replied robotically drifting into my

thoughts again, remembering my recent failure. The cool car air was growing stale and becoming warmer and well travelled. My breaths puffed out with anticipation of a rest.

My memory took me back. When his parents had asked him the question we're all asked, Shoal had taken one look at me and scowled. We had known each other from classes at school, but even then I had never said much to him. His blonde hair, curly and soft, always fell into his eyes when he spoke and I had always wanted to reach out and brush it away. I could always spot a Mer, even if they sensed no magic in me. For some reason I sensed it better than most, probably because of my empathic abilities, something akin to a dolphin's echolocation. It also helped that he was taller than the rest of the boys in our grade and already building muscle. My suspicion was confirmed when I learned he lived close to an outpost.

Shoal was attractive, but I knew what he thought of me. Mer ritual dictated that both parties, had to agree to the betrothal, that way parents couldn't be blamed later for an unhappy match.

"You don't even look like a Mer," he had said accusingly. "How could I accept a betrothal?"

My parents were disheartened by his response, but it was what I had expected. It was what I always heard. It was the truth. At least that time I had not been forced to voice my acceptance of him prior to his clear refusal. I learned from my past mistakes. I looked nothing like a Mer.

We'd left the mildness of the west coast, driving endlessly to the other side of the country, and now I expected the same rejection again. I had been to Nova Scotia when I was much younger and liked it very much. Although the name of my new home made me optimistic, I had serious doubts about it bringing me any luck. Located along the cove and inlets of the Atlantic, Seabright, was a small village, filled with beauty from what I could see in photos.

As we turned up the steep driveway and towards our new home I realized that our house was much nicer than I had imagined. Clearly an older home with Victorian features and large windows reflecting the view, it had been built alongside the rural highway and overlooking a stretch of water. I gazed down the long curving road, stretched out farther than my eyes would see. I knew that this place would be peaceful. Maybe here I could mend my Mer soul, so devastatingly weakened from countless rejections.

Chapter 2

I AWOKE THE NEXT day to a cold November morning. My eyes, small slits, peered over to my window seat and up to the glass square leaking light into the otherwise dark room. Leftover droplets from last night's rain were clinging to the large window pane. I was dry as a bone, but would much rather have felt dewy and fresh. December was fast approaching and soon the frost would set in, making swirling patterns from the moisture in the air. I was surprised that the cold had not been much worse than a mild winter day, but that could change quickly.

I was warm in my cocoon of sheets, but I knew the moment that I threw them off the morning chill would wake me and rouse my thirst. I sat up so that I could grab the glass on the nightstand and drained its contents before my feet hit the ground.

My mother had always insisted that I look my best before greeting any day. How I was supposed to accomplish that I didn't know, but nevertheless I stood before my mirror and grabbed my brush. My hair was short and wiry, tangled so hopelessly that I always fought with what looked more like a rat's nest. Mermaids were supposed to have long silken hair, and mine looked nothing of the sort. Dark brown strands hung in an unruly bob and I puffed out air, frustrated by my lack of progress.

    My eyes narrowed observing every feature, stopping on my predominant eyebrows. I didn't really have eyebrows, I had *an* eyebrow, of dark coarse hair, which I refused to let my mother anywhere near with a pair of tweezers. Countless times, she had said it would only take a few moments to rectify the unibrow, but the pain I knew it would inflict made me shy away. Not even her soothing songs could calm me long enough for the task. On her most recent attempt she had followed me around the kitchen, pestering me until at last my father, looking up from his newspaper, interrupted our squabble and said, "My love, leave our poor daughter alone."

    She had looked wounded for a fragment of a second before hugging me close. "Oh Anya, you're growing so fast." She said tucking me under her arm. I had wanted to groan loudly. I wasn't a kid anymore- despite being trapped in this awful body- and she knew. My mind far surpassed my appearance.

    I stared at the reflection of my lanky limbs and remembered what it felt like to hug my mother. She was curvaceous and cuddly, while I was barely visible, skeletal almost. Clearly not the way to be to attract a male Mer. I needed to eat more, but it didn't matter how much I loved food and that I ate almost the same amount as my father; my weight never seemed to change.

Often, I felt I should blame my human genes. Scientifically, it was the only thing that could be keeping me from transcendence. Where most Mers my age had their lustrous locks already grown in, their skin scaled- then cleared, and their shapes filled in to the naturally fleshy Mer frame. I had done none of that, with not even a hint of Mer powers or Mer physical characteristics on the horizon.

I realized how hungry I was after examining my scraggly frame . I threw on a pair of purple fuzzy slippers and made my way down to the kitchen, picking at my braces freshly cleaned with toothpaste. Luckily the braces were only needed to straighten my existing teeth, which exhibited the same strong density as other Mers. Thankfully, I could soon have them removed.

Descending the wooden staircase, my ears perked each time I set foot on a creaky spot and I knew by nightfall I would have memorized the correct moves to make to avoid them in the future. My fingers ran along the wooden banister, enjoying the smooth waxen feeling of its polished surface.

I found my parents in the kitchen; my mother spooning our food onto plates while my father filled our glasses with juice. They were a team, and tackled even the simplest tasks together, including what I had nicknamed their pet science projects. According to them, it was serious work. It employed them and paid for our family expenses so I understood it had to be something worthwhile. To me, it seemed like mystic work that was never discussed above a level of a subtle whisper.

"Anya, after breakfast you have to get dressed. We're going over to the Price's to meet the suitor." I had barely sat in the stool by the counter before the words left my mother's mouth, hope gleaming in my father's eyes.

The newest suitor had been brought to my parent's attention by the head of scientific Mer research at the Halifax outpost. Arturo, a college friend who had attended school with my father in the deep blue, had explained that the Price family were having a hard time finding a Mer their son would accept for betrothal. Why Arturo had considered me I didn't understand, especially since science and warrior families rarely intermixed in Mer communities. Arturo had visited us only a few months prior and knew exactly what I was like...and what I looked like. Why he thought the Price family would want me, I didn't know. My mouth flew open in shock. We had been there less than twenty four hours and already I was being taken to yet another match-making meeting.

"So soon?" I asked closing my mouth to a twist and digging my fork into my salmon and eggs. The fleshy textures on my tongue were perfectly flavoured and I savoured them before I swallowed and took a cool drink of iced water.

"Yes," my father replied, "the Prices requested we meet as soon as possible.

My mother smiled at him and then at me. "Anya, we think it's a good sign."

I wanted to grumble, and sulk, and sink off of my seat to the floor, but instead I simply nodded, preparing myself for the usual rejection. It didn't take long to eat. I had lost my appetite.

I soaked in the tub for as long as I could and then returned to my room to dress. I knew what I would have to wear. I owned one black dress, which in my eyes was one dress too many. It was cotton and simple, and far too big. My flat chest made the scoop neckline look deflated and the skirt fell straight down way below my knees to a length completely unappealing and almost dowdy. At least the three quarter length sleeves did some good at hiding the lankiness of my arms. I placed a red headband in my hair for some colour and pulled out the cherry lip balm I always wore for these types of occasions. My mother always wore lip gloss and bold shades of lipstick. Staring at my seemingly pale reflection I pondered whether I should ask her for some, maybe even some in red.

    P<small>ULLING UP TO THE</small> Prices' home I started to get the usual nervous feeling in the pit of my stomach. I had been through this same process a million times over. The parents always met in a room while I waited, bored, in some other part of the home. Then I would be beckoned in for the suitor to see and three minutes later we would be on our way home.
    The white house looked neat and simple. It looked like many of the other houses on this stretch of road. Its long driveway was straight and adjacent to the left side of the house. The green grass made my eyes travel upwards and past the few garden beds dotted with wild flowers to the green shutters framing all of the windows- large windows that looked like seal eyes, ominous and black.
    When we arrived, there were three teenage girls sitting on the front porch. Two of the girls seemed close to me in age while the third was clearly older. I suddenly wondered if I would be there to compete and if so, wondered what fighting chance I would have considering they all had shining long hair, beautiful skin, and complimentary pastel coloured dresses. They rose to their feet as my family had approached with broad smiles on their faces.

"You must be Anya," the tallest spoke, looking at me with curiosity. Her blonde hair was pale and straight, set off by the deep blue of her eyes. She wore the simplest dress of the three, a straight lavender shift dress with a tie at the waist.

"Kanja." My father spoke his name extending his hand for the girl to mimic the gesture. Their fingers never touched, but they sensed one another this way, it was customary for our people.

"Raisa." My mother said, her Russian accent thick, repeating the gesture of my father.

"Rayne." The tall girl said at last, "we are Merrick's sisters, and would like to keep Anya company while you meet with our parents."

My parents looked at me, their eyes asking if I would be alright. I nodded quickly, immediately appreciating the gesture the girls offered. Far more often I was left alone in a room for close to an hour while plans and details were discussed. I grew smart enough to bring a book with me out of habit, but still I much preferred reading in the comfort of my own spaces. I smiled to reassure them, and at last they left joining Ondine and Caspian, the parents of my suitor who introduced themselves to me quickly before ushering my parents along in haste.

"Our brother is so difficult," the smallest one started. Her wavy blonde hair was long and bobbed in the breeze while her green eyes brightened. The ruffles in the peach coloured skirt of her dress were flowing like seaweed with a tide. "It is taking him forever to choose a mate."

"Shh Coral, you'll make her nervous," the third spoke, clearly the middle sister of the three. Her hair was chestnut brown, blue eyes piercing as they shot towards me. Her dress similar to Corals was a bit less ornate and pearly blue in hue.

"Well he is!" Coral exclaimed.

"I'm already nervous," I admitted honestly. "I usually am for the first few minutes, but it passes."

"Sorry," she winced.

Rayne laughed. "Pearl, you're so sweet," she said to her sister, "why couldn't you give Merrick some of your kindness? You *are* his twin." Pearl merely scoffed in reply.

My fingers twined nervously and Pearl reached out to calm them.

"They're giving you the wrong impression. He's not cruel."

"No!" Coral added, "He's just a male."

Rayne laughed.

Pearl smiled sweetly. "I think he'll like you," she spoke in earnest.

"I doubt that," the words spilling out of me before I thought about them.

"He would be a good mate to you, even though he's a bugger of a brother," Coral added.

Rayne looked at me scrutinizing and her eyes fell to the book in my hand.

"You're just his type too."

And then, I grew more nervous, but for completely different reasons. They seemed convinced that their brother, Merrick, would in a few moments choose me for his future bride. I had arrived fully anticipating a rejection and so the glimmer of hope sparking through me was completely foreign. It felt like I was about to be betrayed. The outcome still unknown, suddenly I wanted to run down to the beach and hide away somewhere along the shore.

Before I could speak another word, a young male Mer popped out of the door. He was slightly shorter than me, with messy blonde hair and the same blue eyes as the older female Mers. He wore a black suit and a navy tie, as formally dressed as his siblings. I wondered. Was this Merrick? They had said he was Pearl's not Coral's twin, and he looked far more like Coral. He also looked younger than me, but similarly scraggly. He was cute in his own way, but perhaps a bit young looking for me to find attractive.

"Come with me," he said grabbing my hand and urging me from the porch bench. His glance was scrutinizing, but pleasant and he was smiling easily.

"It's time," Rayne said with a wink. I looked back at the sisters helplessly while my potential betrothed dragged me along.

As we walked through the corridor I observed the details of the Prices' home. It was quite beautiful and refreshing, a nautical theme adorning every wall. The walls were a robin's egg blue and white wainscoting and trim seemed to be everywhere. Merrick led me towards a closed door and I swallowed hard. Suddenly I was craving water. Would our parents be disappointed if either of us hesitated? He pushed open the door to reveal my parents with Ondine and Caspian, all sitting on a cream sofa set. My parents were sitting next to one another on a couch, while Ondine was draped over Caspian on a facing loveseat- his arm wrapped over her shoulder. My eyes quickly scanned, curved mirrors and frosted glass sculptures decorated the room; a bronze cast mermaid hung on the wall. How ironic.

"Thank you Zale," Ondine spoke, "you may leave now." He squeezed my hand tighter and looked at me as though he did not want to leave before finally letting go.

Zale? Was that not Merrick?

I felt confused, and my palms grew sweaty with anxiety, my left hand still tightly wrapped around my book, felt it slipping and I shifted it to my other hand.

The sharp hitch of the door closing behind me made me jump, but I smiled at the Prices to smooth away signs of my apprehension.

"You look lovely Anya." Caspian spoke, a broad smile on his lips revealing perfect white teeth. I fought the urge to glance at my parents with an 'Is he serious?' look.

"Don't you think, Merrick?" Ondine asked and glanced over her shoulder to the window behind the sofas.

My eyes followed hers and my breath caught when they found the object of her questioning. Merrick was definitely a Mer. He was leaning against the window, a sheer curtain billowing behind him, poised like some old film star. I wanted to pinch myself awake.

His chestnut brown hair fell below his jaw line in soft shiny strands. His eyes were the same deep blue as his siblings, but something about them shimmered in the light, flickering with green and making them appear teal. His face was handsome in the model sort of way, but rugged, with a strong jawline and dark brows. His shoulders were broad and his build -muscular despite being only a few years my senior- made me feel a bit too small in comparison.

Clearly, he had already undergone his transcendence. His eyes moved over me slowly and I had a gripping fear that my girlish frame of bones would displease him. If it did, he gave no indication, not even a flicker in his eye suggested disappointment.

"Yes she does," he spoke, in a resonant and rich voice that drew a shiver down my spine. Then he added, without batting an eyelash, "I accept her as my betrothed."

My body twitched up, straightening as I watched

his parents faces fill with pure joy and astonishment. Not so much astonishment at me, for they didn't look at me as other parents had, but more in the sense of satisfaction that their son had finally chosen another Mer – at last. Their faces were riddled with relief.

I looked at my parents suddenly unsure of what to do. They met my glances encouragingly and had they been able to, I'm sure they would have shouted for me that I gladly accepted Merrick too. They had been waiting a long time for this day as well, but it was my choice. I would have to say the words.

My voice seemed to fail me and I pulled my book closer to my chest, both hands now gripping the paperback cover. My breath was hot and came out ragged. All eyes in the room fell upon me, awaiting the words they longed to hear. I looked at Merrick again.

What was it about me that made him decide so quickly? We hadn't even spoken a word alone, which was customary. He didn't look bored, or like he was joking. I had no idea what his motive was, yet, I knew a chance like this would not come again. Should I not take this opportunity I might end up an old sea hag or even worse a siren. My mouth wanted to twist in thought before speaking, but my silence had already been too much. The added gesture might insult the Mer-god of a male standing before me.

"I accept Merrick as my betrothed," I said. The words sticky in my mouth like honey. His arms, which had crossed in the interim of waiting, fell to his sides with relief, the tension in his flexing muscles faded.

I couldn't believe that he had picked me and I stood there waiting for someone to say 'Surprise it's a pre-birthday joke!' or better yet, for me to wake up from a ridiculous dream. It didn't happen though, and the rest of the visit was filled with customary pleasantries. Our parents spoke about a few minor things like the due date for our marriage, which had thankfully been set for our early twenties and not our late teens as many parents usually advocated. They discussed whether or not we would each attend college.

Merrick and I did not exchange a single word, but when my father spoke on my behalf, stating that I would definitely be studying further after high school, Merrick's eyes lit up with a twinge of amusement and looked over at me. I sensed it was approval, but it was hard to tell without watching him closer. I did not want to let on that I desperately wanted to examine him.

We left not long after that, and after eating supper that night, I felt emotionally drained. Peeling off my black dress I folded it on top of my laundry pile and crawled into bed. The same book I had brought with me to the Price's that day was firmly clasped in between my fingers while my eyes wandered over the pages. I didn't read- could not- simply looked at the words while my mind hazed over thoughts of Merrick. I would one day be his wife, and the thought had sent jolts of feeling through me: first excitement; then apprehension; and then, complete fear.

When would I see him again? Would we have a chance to actually speak? What were his likes and dislikes? Did he read books?

My body was anxious and my mind weary, but I had to sleep since the next day would be my first day of school. I let the book fall from my hands and turned to make a muffled scream into my pillow. I prayed that the following day would be a good one, since this one had been completely unnerving.

Chapter 3

THE HOUSE HAD ALREADY been cleaned and assembled, most of the boxes unpacked and organized. My parents' telekinetic powers always helped them accomplish things quickly. Telekinesis was popular among the science Mers and was something I had yet to experience. I wanted to be capable of the same talent and had anticipated its arrival any day since I was ten. The same age each of my parents discovered their powers. Now at thirteen I accepted that perhaps it might never happen.

My parents worked long hours, they always had. They went in early and came home late, especially more recently. Now that I was older they knew I could fend for myself and I honestly didn't mind the time to be alone.

I woke early from a fitful sleep. The night had me filled with dreams. Over and over, I saw Merrick's mouth stretched in a wide smile. At one point, we were sitting on a rock by the shore watching a moonlit sky. He then beckoned for me to join him in the water running towards its rushing roar. Before I knew it, he was swimming out into the inky black waves; rays of light from the moon cascading down over the ripples. He transformed into the most breathtaking Merman I had ever seen. I watched his shimmering scales flicker against the surface of the water, fog lifting off the water from the heat in his body. The essence emanating from him pulled me to him. Projected outside of myself, I watched as I ran to him laughing, my body slowly shifting to scales when my feet grew wet. I glimmered as I ran further over the silver sand and my hair was long and silken. I dove into the waves swimming quickly after him while he called my name; and just before I reached him, I woke.

    I sighed, surprised I had even dreamed, with so few hours of true rest. At least the extra time had allowed me to soak in the bath for longer. I sank beneath the surface for as long as I could, blowing bubbles one at a time for them to float to the surface. When at last I knew my time was running short and I needed to leave the house, I begrudgingly got out and towelled off.

    Once dressed in my blue jeans and plain black sweater I glanced in the mirror before throwing on my black scarf, coat, and gloves. I slipped on my boots and walked out the door, locking it behind me. The cooler outdoor air greeted me freshly.

    I had always disliked school, despite my good grades and ability to blend into the crowds unseen. There was something about being closed off in small rooms with a bunch of other people my age, all frustrated, or eager, or nonchalant that made me uneasy with which vibe I should adopt myself. I usually ended up with the overachievers, simply because I was generally calm and no one else would accept me as their own.

I walked down to the bus stop and waited. There were two girls there who were busy staring at their phones while texting. I smiled at them and they nodded back before I was once again ignored. A sporty looking red car drove speedily around the bend and then jerked to slow down. I spotted Rayne as she deftly pulled the vehicle to the shoulder of the highway. It was a full car, Pearl and Coral were seated in the back with a male Mer that I assumed was the betrothed of one of them. Merrick had shotgun in front; his eyes locked onto me through the glass. Rayne rolled the window down with a quick press of a button and as soon as Merrick was revealed in plain sight, instantly the girls behind me could be heard giggling. My instincts would have had me groaning at them, but instead I smiled politely leaning towards the car.

"Hey!" Rayne said, "Hop in!"

"Ummmm," I said my face twisting in confusion. "There's no room," I said with a light laugh.

"You can sit on Merrick's lap. We have to drop Coral off at middle school anyway, so you can sit in the back after." She replied as if all had been solved. The girls behind me had gasped in shock.

His expression didn't change, there was no disgust or annoyance, but he hadn't opened the door and gestured me onto his lap. Plus there was the concern of safety.

"She doesn't want to Raynestorm," Merrick replied, his rich voice even and matter of fact.

"Don't call me that Merbear!" She said with a swat at his arm.

The yellow school bus pulled in front of the stop and I gestured toward it with my hand. "It's ok the bus is here. See you at school!" I didn't give her time to protest. I waved goodbye and ran up the steps before the doors closed.

"Well you're new!" The driver exclaimed, his eyes brightening with his smile.

"Hi, I'm Anya," I said offering my hand. He took it and shook it firmly.

"Pleased to meet you miss. I'm Rodney, your bus driver. Help yourself to a seat."

"Thanks," I said hoping I had not been too awkward. I sat in the next available place sinking into the squeaky leatherette upholstered cushion. The drive was scenic and the blur of trees and pebbled beaches were breathtaking. The warmth of the fall leaves in orange, yellow, and red stood out against the sparkling blue surface on the coves glinting white above the teal depths. Even the rocky beaches were stained with similar autumn tones and dotted with rust coloured algae and rich green and mustard seaweed. The beauty had me feeling awakened and inspired, ready for more exploration of my new home.

    The bus arrived at school well after the Prices did. As I walked up, I spotted their car parked in the lot, but they were nowhere to be seen. I kind of wished that I had gone with them. It would have been nice to have arrived on my first day with friends, but it was too late now.

The school was an impressive building. By its architecture, it had been built in more recent years. The long wall of windows and steel were modern, and it was interesting to watch people move in the reflective surface. It was a smaller high school of about a four hundred students. It felt cold though, institutional as most schools always had. It was easy enough to navigate though and my first few classes went by quickly.

All of the teachers instantly recognized me as the new girl. They were kind though, and thankfully my science teacher had sat me next to a girl named Leah. She was friendly and invited me to sit with her and her friend, Evelyn, at lunch time. I was grateful for her kindness as I had no idea if I would even see the Mers at lunch. It would also save me the awkward, "Can I sit with you?" conversation, which had happened to me countless times before. I hadn't seen the Mers all day, probably since they were all in older grades.

The cafeteria was like any other school cafeteria, and even before Leah, Evelyn and I were seated, I could see why the Mers probably wouldn't come here and why they were nowhere in sight. The lights were too bright, and the dull buzz of the sound speaker was a droning annoyance. It was modern and very spacious, but something about it was grating to my inner Mermaid.

By the end of the day I was truly ready to go home. Other than introductions and discussing what I had understood of the material I had missed, not much had been accomplished in any of my classes. It turned out that I hadn't missed much and would be able to pick things up rather quickly, but I still couldn't wait to curl up with a good book on my window seat. I took the bus home, again unable to find the Mers and not wanting to assume the offer would be made for a drive home.

BY MID-WEEK THE overwhelming newness of everything had finally dulled to routine. Evelyn and Leah invited me to go shopping with them for the

Christmas formal coming up in December. They asked me if I planned to go, but being new to the school and not liking to wear dresses I wasn't sure just yet. Apparently shopping early was the best way to ensure no one else had the same dress, which to me didn't seem like it would be the end of the world.

Leah's mom had driven us to Bayer's Lake to check out the outlets there and we were trekking from store to store in search of something suitable for their sparkling personalities.

"What about purple?" Evelyn held up a purple dress with a black lace overlay. It was actually really pretty, with a sweetheart neckline on the dress underneath. She could tell I liked it, but I merely shrugged feeling that I definitely did not have the figure to fill it out. It might look like a bag on me, even in the smallest size. I was definitely not keen on attending, but then I thought about Merrick and wondered if he would be going to the school dance. If he went though, would he even want to dance with me?

Evelyn passed the sales associate her items and slipped into a fitting room. I sighed waiting outside while Leah joined her in the fun, trying on garments in an adjacent room.

"I don't really think I am going to go to the dance, you guys," I said while they wrestled into their gowns.

Leah gasped, coming out of the fitting room. Her short auburn curls bobbed as she jerked back.

"No! You have to come!" She grabbed my arm. Her pale green eyes intensified as they fixated on me. She was wearing a knee length teal dress which had a halter neckline and a jewelled collar. It looked magnificent on her.

Evelyn came out of her room and pushed her black glasses higher onto the bridge of her nose, her long black hair was pulled high in a bun and it looked cute with the strapless plum coloured dress she wore. It was set off by her beige complexion and dark brown eyes like mine.

"I wish you would come with us Anya, but I understand if you don't want to." She smiled at me and then continued, "what do you think?" She asked in a singsong voice. She seemed to be ignoring Leah's outburst and her button nose wrinkled in sympathy for me. She and I were very relaxed, so we seemed to even out Leah's intense emotions.

"I think it looks great," I said.

"Oh I'm so jealous of your complexions, you two," Leah said with a pout.

My first instinct was to laugh since her expression was so dramatically martyred, but instead I was sympathetic.

"You have beautiful skin," I said to her.

"Yeah, but you two have a natural tan all year long. I have to go to a tanning bed for that and even then, I burn first before I get just a little bit darker."

Evelyn shook her head laughing. "Yeah well maybe in the next lifetime your mom will be Filipino."

Leah stuck her tongue out at her. The thought of a tanning bed made me want to squirm. Anything that would dry me out would be unpleasant.

"What's your mix Anya?" Evelyn asked shifting the dress and trying on a necklace the sales woman had brought over.

"My father is from India. My mother is from Russia." I felt like we were bonding over our parentage and it was actually pretty fun to be sharing these tidbits about myself that no one usually cared to ask.

"Nice, but you were born in Canada right?" Evie said. I nodded.

Leah sighed. "Your dad looks like Oded Fehr. Dreamy!"

"How do you know what my dad looks like?" I asked surprised by her proclamation.

Leah was playing with her curls, messily placing them atop her head as she spoke. "My mom owns the bakery in Upper Tantallon and he stopped there the other day. I knew he was your dad immediately. It was pretty clear once he said, my daughter Anya loves chocolate."

"Oh," I said with a smile, "yeah, I guess my dad's a good looking guy." Both of my parents were very attractive... and then there was me. I couldn't help but glance in the mirrors in front of me and wish that I looked more like a Mermaid. I took a seat and flipped through a nearby magazine to keep myself distracted.

In the next hour they must have each tried on over half a dozen dresses, but when they were finished they had finally found their choices. Leah ended up with a robin's egg blue halter dress, similar to her first choice while Evelyn opted for a notched orange strapless dress. Even though I hadn't bought anything for myself I still managed to walk out of the store with a shopping high. Part of me was a little convinced that *just maybe* school dances could become my sort of thing.

Chapter 4

THE FIRST WEEK OF school went quickly and by the end of it, the buzz of the cafeteria dulled and my eyes had adjusted to the bright lights. The morning bus rides were not nearly as bad as they could have been, and I was completely caught up on the important material I missed so far in the term. I had been so busy with studying and spending time in the library during the week that I hadn't really seen much of the Price family, or had the time to introduce myself to any of the other Mers who attended Sir John A Macdonald High School.

There weren't any science Mers aside from me; the rest of them lived in Halifax and attended high school there. It seemed that only my parents had strayed from the rest of them and rented a more rural house.

Now that I had handed in the first few projects and assignments for all of my classes though, I felt as though I had a little time to relax. It had been a peaceful Saturday of reading and making shell jewellery. I had cleaned the shells collected the previous weekend and prepared them for a pair of earring hooks when my mother burst into my room on the phone.

"Yes I'll tell her," she said her eyes falling on me. "Oh of course, Ondine, I agree with you completely... actually, would you like to speak with her?"

That anxious feeling I always got when my mother passed me the phone started to surface, and I was relieved when she said, "no? Okay, I'll tell her," and hung up the receiver. "You've been invited to spend time with Merrick this Sunday." My mother said looking at me proudly.

"Oh?" I said unsure of how to react. "Okay."

"The Prices are going to Moncton for a shopping trip and Merrick doesn't want to go. The drive's about three hours, too long for him. Ondine and Caspian thought you might keep him company."

I let the words sink in. "I'm going to be alone with him!?"

My mom laughed. "Why do you sound so fearful? He's from an honourable family." She leaned against my window seat.

"Mother, I hardly know the guy."

"You'll be fine," she said with a smile, "you know what we Mers are like Anya, just be yourself. He's your betrothed. He won't harm you. In fact, he's magically bound to protect you."

"What does dad think?" I knew better than to try and pit one parent against the other. I rarely did as my parents were devoted to each other, always respecting one another's opinions.

"Your father approves," she said smiling and then patted me on the head before leaving. I let out a deep sigh. Well at least this way we would finally talk with each other.

I ARRIVED AT THE Price house at 1:50 PM. The same seal-eyed windows on the house spoke to me, only this time they appeared much less ominous, familiar almost.

"Have a good time!" My father said with a smile.

"You're not coming in?" I asked nervously. He shook his head.

I got out of the car and puffed out a deep breath, while I swung my father's vintage satchel over my shoulder. I had convinced him to give it to me for my birthday. The brown leatherette was soft as I ran my fingers over it before ringing the doorbell. My father was still waiting in the car, and I was thankful that at least he was going to make sure Merrick was there. The door swung open a few seconds later, and he stepped out onto the patio waving to my father, who honked the horn a few times before he pulled away.

"Hi," I said, feeling shy as he ushered me in and I removed my boots.

"Hey Anya," he said, the corner of his mouth pulling upwards slightly when he noticed me shift uncomfortably. His eyes examined me from head to toe and back.

"So..." I said, not really sure what else to say.

"Is that all you brought for a jacket?" He asked

"Yes. Why?" I asked, noticing that he only wore a long sleeved white tee beneath an opened plaid shirt with a pair of jeans. Ondine hadn't mentioned that I would need to dress any particular way, so I just wore jeans and a black sweater with my regular fall pea coat and scarf.

"I need to work on my bike in the garage for a little bit. Are you hungry, thirsty?" He asked gesturing for me to come further into the house.

"No, I ate already," I replied, though I had been so nervous and had to force my my food down.

"Good," he said stopping by the foot of the stairs to button up his shirt. I watched him button the first few, his dark hair was falling into his eyes and he looked incredibly cute, his mouth twisting with charm. My eyes were fixed on him until he glanced up at me and I slowly turned my head, and made my eyes examine the room.

He smirked at me, and I tried looking innocent before I asked, "what?"

"You're going to need another coat kiddo?"

One of my eyebrows shot up into an arch. "Kiddo?"

"Yeah," he said coming closer and flicking my nose. "Kiddo. Come on, follow me upstairs." I was annoyed by his flippant attitude, and by the fact that he had flicked my nose, but I still managed to follow.

We made our way to his room, which was surprisingly clean. My eyes examined quickly. I was impressed. Unlike the rest of the house, Merrick's room was quite the contrast. The wainscoting in his room was a medium stained wood, not the stark white in the rest of the house. The grain and texture of it popped against midnight blue walls. One wall was decorated with framed canvases. Each had been splattered with iridescent blue and green paint, and the centre one etched was with a human heart.

His things were placed neatly on bookshelves: many books, and some board games. A double bed with a medium stained wooden frame was in the middle of the room, a plaid comforter neatly spread out over its surface. The nightstands at his bedside had large, amber coloured, glass lamps with rustic grasscloth lampshades. One lamp was turned on, spilling light over the surface of the right table where a chess set had been placed. All of its pieces were in their appropriate spots on the board except for a sole white knight lying toppled to its side—defeated maybe.

He opened the closet door and riffled through it to the back.

"This should do," he said pulling an item out and tossing it to me. It was a quilted jacket that would be huge on me. I popped open the snaps and slipped it on. It smelled like cologne and grease. Thankfully more like the former than the latter. I was tempted to pull the collar up so I could smell it more deeply, but he was looking at me in consideration while he slipped into a similar jacket. My fingers fumbled under his scrutiny and he closed the distance between us, buttoning the snaps for me.

"You're a bag of bones," he said with a nod towards my mid section, "you need to eat more."

"Believe me, I eat plenty," I said without thinking and finished the top two buttons before he could. My fingers still trembled a little, feeling rushed and uneasy with his presence. Of course, he noticed.

"Are you afraid of me, little mouse?" He asked leaning in even more so that I backed up until I was flush against the door. His arm pushed back against the door until it closed. The sound of the latch closed with a resonant echo on my burning ears. My nose and mouth were covered by the tall collar of the coat, but if I could see my eyes I imagined they were as big as sand dollars. Then I realized what he had just called me and my temper reared.

"Must you insult me!?" I said pulling down the collar to project my voice. "First I'm kiddo, then a bag of bones, and now a mouse! Honestly do you think I'm just a little child? I won't always look like this!" He still looked at me thoughtfully. "By Poseidon, I pray I don't."

"At least my little mouse has a voice," he said amused, and then slid me to the side of the door to open it and hastily make for the stairs. He sauntered down them with grace until he disappeared.

"Come on Anya." He called from the bottom of them returning to see where I was.

I groaned to myself, but followed him, slipping on my boots and walking after him to their shed. As soon as we were outside I was glad that he had given me an extra jacket.

He flicked on the halogen lights and the dark room brightened enough for me to see all of the tools and empty cans about. If he kept his room tidy, his workplace was quite the mess in contrast. The wood smell was pleasantly strong, tinged only slightly by grease and some sort of mild chemical or adhesive.

"You can sit there," he said pointing to an upside down barrel. It didn't look very sturdy, but I took his word for it and sat down gingerly. I pulled out my gloves from my bag and the book I had brought in case he decided to ignore me until my parents came to get me.

I started reading, only glancing at him on the rare occasion when he cursed, frustrated by what he was doing. I didn't ask if things were okay because clearly, they weren't. Although the words rested on the tip of my tongue, they never came out. Instead I paused from my reading to watch him until he seemed to figure everything out and began to work again.

About forty-five minutes into our little routine he stopped working and looked up. My foot had been jiggling. It was partly because the part in the book that

I had gotten too was exciting and I didn't know what would happen next and partly because it was colder than usual. I didn't handle the cold as well as other Mers unless it was in water. Somehow he guessed.

"Are you cold?" He asked me.

I looked up over the top of my book. "A little."

He pulled out a space heater, planting it near my legs, and turned it on, adding to the vibrating noises in the room as the machine hummed out heat.

"Ooo toasty," I said. "Thank you." I jiggled my feet in front of it, until at last, I felt warmed. We continued in the same fashion- him working, and me reading for another thirty minutes before he stopped altogether.

"Anya," he said and waited until I looked at him before he continued. "Are you going to talk to me at all?"

I placed my bookmark in my book and let it rest in my lap considering his question carefully.

He wanted to talk? Why hadn't I gotten that impression?

"You want to talk?" I asked trying to hide my surprise. "What do you want to talk about?"

"I dunno," he answered averting my gaze. "Isn't that what we're supposed to be doing here? Is there anything you want to know about me? Is there anything you want to ask?"

There were a million things I wanted to know about him, but only one question I really wanted to ask.

"Anything?" I asked, this time my eyes were fixed on him. Even though he didn't waver, I could detect a slight uneasiness in his emotions.

"Yep," he replied, his teal eyes meeting mine. I took a deep breath, preparing the words in my mind before I spoke them.

"Why did you pick me? We hadn't spoken a word and you chose me for your mate?" We would remain bound to each other forever, but this part I did not add- neither of us needed the reminder.

"Honestly?" He began, walking closer to me as though it were a secret. He remained quiet, so I nodded to encourage him.

"I figured I had more time to spare since you're the youngest candidate I've met. I mean, you haven't transcended yet, and you're intelligent. You probably recognize that some of this is pretty archaic. Sure our parents seem pretty happy, but sometimes I wonder if they really think that we'll be satisfied with spending eons together if we don't see other people while we're young to figure out what we like- to experience life. I understand we'll have the rest of our lives together, eventually, but right now we're young. We should have fun."

I wasn't disappointed with his answer. It was rational, well thought out and well said. He continued to move closer as I began to speak.

"Makes sense," I replied, "I understand then. I was glad that we both agreed at the first meeting that education is important and that will take time. And really it's not like I look like a Mer just yet anyway, so I knew you weren't instantly attracted to me since I'm no bathing beauty, so to speak. You're not really the first Mer who didn't find me attractive anyway. At least now I understand your motive and then like you say we can just figure things out eventually. Although, I would understand if you change your mind, Merrick, I'm not really much of a Mer yet so don't feel like you have to—"

And then he kissed me. His soft lips pressed against mine tenderly while his scent invaded my nostrils. It was not just once either, but three successive, sweet kisses while his hand wrapped around my cheek.

I had closed my eyes savouring each kiss- kissing him back just as softly, and when I opened them I looked at him, confused. After everything he had just said—he kissed me.

"Why did you do that?" My eyes were searching his veiled facial expression.

"You were talking too much." He said simply.

"Oh. Sorry." I said and swallowed hard, my heart hammering up to my throat.

"Just don't do it again," he warned. And I wondered if it would grant me more kisses to keep rambling on like a fool. Suddenly I thought that I might want more kisses, or did I? I didn't speak, instead I nodded.

He returned to his bike and tinkered for a few minutes before he lifted it, placed in a corner and threw his tools on the counter.

"It's too cold out now. We should head back inside." He said opening the shed door for me.

I hopped down from the barrel, returned my book to my bag and turned off the heater before following him. I was still a little confused by the kisses. There was no pity in his eyes, or attraction... maybe curiosity. Yes, perhaps he had kissed me out of curiosity, but even that didn't seem to add up and his emotions were so unclear.

Chapter 5

As soon as we made it inside, I felt as though it was too warm. The intimacy between us made my heart tingle and I didn't know how to feel about it all. He grabbed the jacket from my hand, hanging it with his on a rack by the door and we made our way to the kitchen. As he grabbed a box of mac and cheese from the cupboard, I grimaced inwardly.

"You're not going to eat that are you?" I asked.

He gave me a mischievous look. "Umm yeah, unless you want to make me something better."

I couldn't help but chuckle. "Put that back, I'll make you something better."

Then I was looking through the cupboards, asking him where things were and assembling ingredients on the counter. Since my parents were rarely home during the week to make supper, I learned early on how to cook, and usually prepared something for them.

"Do you have any shrimp?" I asked him while I diced a tomato and placed it next to the already chopped garlic clove. He had watched me with a hint of amazement as I had moved around the kitchen, and a single finger shot up bidding me to wait while he disappeared into a pantry. He returned with fresh shrimp, scallops, and clams. My mouth watered immediately.

"Won't your parents need that for your family meals?" I asked not wanting to use up too much of their food supply.

Merrick chuckled. "No, you should see the fresh fish on ice in the cold room, plus the freezer in there, it's filled with seafood. They won't mind, we usually rifle through it as we please."

"Oh," I said suddenly wondering what it would be like to have a much larger family, to even have siblings.

I cooked quickly, while he watched and grabbed me anything I needed. Soon the sauce I was preparing was done. I grabbed the linguine I had found and added it to the boiling pot.

"You must cook often," he said leaning against the counter still watching me.

"Yeah, I do," I said picking up the spoon to stir the sauce.

"Let me taste that," he said with a smile handing me a smaller spoon. I scooped some up blowing on it lightly to cool it and he moved closer, bending down with his mouth slightly ajar.

"Mmm," he said, his lips smacking in approval. "It's really good but it needs some hot sauce. Do you like your food spicy?" He asked me.

"Yeah, sometimes," I replied grabbing the hot

sauce I had spotted in the fridge and adding a few drops.

"Will you make me supper like this when we're married?" He asked.

My cheeks flushed as I realized what he said. *When we're married?*

My thoughts suddenly muddled. It seemed like such a faraway place in time.

I wandered off to that time and place, but only for a few extra seconds before I finally found my voice, "Yes, most of the time."

He leaned in closer to me, still bracing against the counter. "You'll spoil me." He said smiling.

I smiled back while I drained the pasta, but then gave him a sharp look. "Sometimes you're going to have to help me and other times you'll have to cook -not anything out of a box either."

He crossed his arms, but leaned back in relaxation. "Alright Anya, but you'll have to teach me how to cook first."

I assembled the noodles and sauce on his plate, cutting up fresh green onions and pulling out some grated parmesan to sprinkle over the top.

"That I can do," I said.

He disappeared into the dining room and I turned to assemble my own plate hearing him enter behind me and shuffle around in the kitchen before leaving again. Finally finished with my pile of food- not much less than his- I followed and quickly realized he hadn't turned on a single light. Instead he had lit four candles at the centre of the table and had poured water into wine glasses. It looked romantic and like something from a movie, and suddenly I was feeling flushed again, and remembering the kisses that I had pushed from my mind. When I walked over to my seat he was still standing, and with a seemingly ancient gesture he pulled out my chair for me, taking my plate and placing it on the table.

"You're being a proper gentleman." I said impressed.

"Why not?" He asked finding his seat and eagerly swirling pasta around his fork with a spoon and then skewering a scallop.

"You don't seem the type of Mer to be proper, or a gentleman." I hadn't meant for my tone to be flirtatious, but that was the way it came out. Merrick's eyes flickered with something unrecognizable before he cleared his throat and answered me.

"I'm not always proper or a gentleman, no." He smiled slowly and continued eating. His emotions were still muddled and hard to read. It was then that a thought came hammering through me.

Eventually, we would be married as he had mentioned. He would be my husband and that meant we would make love. Had I been scientific in that moment I would have said that we would have sex, but it seemed like the realization demanded something softer, more romanticized. Truthfully, after all of the books I had read, it was the accurate way I felt about being intimate. I was wistful and hopeful for love.

I might have only been thirteen (turning fourteen at the end of the month) and he fifteen, but in a few years- praying that by then I had transcended, we would both have cycles when we were in heat. Mers were notorious for being incredibly amorous at that time of the month being desirous creatures anyway, past the age of metamorphosis. Yet even then, once we had crossed that line, would he love me?

Merrick paused from eating, noticing that I was deep in thought. "Not hungry?" He asked.

I didn't answer, but immediately started eating. I didn't want to delve into that topic any time soon. Love...sex...either of them too complex.

We watched a movie after supper. A documentary on sharks that I hadn't expected Merrick to want to see. We sat on opposite ends of the couch, our feet meeting in the middle. A couple of times during the film I glanced over to look at him. I wondered what he looked like scaled and if his skin turned the same blue-green like his eyes.

He seemed to feel wary of sharks. As much as I did, although neither of us had met any face to face in the wild. They could be ruthless but for the most part they ate to survive.

The Price family returned home with perfect timing, a few minutes after the movie ended. Even though I had enjoyed my time with Merrick, my mind was now swimming with far too many questions about the future. They were questions that I would have preferred to lock away and revisit at a later time.

Coral, Pearl and Rayne were friendly, giving me each a hug and welcoming me back to their house, though I had been there for the past eight hours.

"Would you like to come up to my room for a few moments?" Pearl asked. Coral was smiling eagerly at her side.

"We could show you all of our great buys before Mom and I take you home," Rayne said while pulling her long blonde hair- now with two streaks of purple in the front- into a ponytail. I glanced over to find Merrick speaking with his younger brother and Caspian, and then I smiled at them with a nod.

"I would love to see all of your new fashion

things."

Rayne and Ondine exchanged a glance of approval, which I guessed had something to do with me looking at Merrick before agreeing to follow them. I wondered if they would ask Merrick about me later that night once I had returned home. They probably would in the same fashion as my parents. For a moment I contemplated what he would say. Would he answer to their questions? Would he tell them he kissed me?

Coral and I sat on the bed, while Pearl sat on her ottoman and Rayne took to the bean bag chair in the corner. They had all bought new winter clothes in an array of pastels and bright colours and I suddenly wondered if those were the type of things that Merrick would want to see me wearing. Truthfully, it wasn't really my style.

"So did you have a good time with Merrick?" Coral asked lying on the bed with her chin propped up on her hands and her feet kicking playfully in the air.

"Of course they had a good time," Rayne said. "Did you spot the leftovers of what Anya must have cooked for him? You spoiled him."

I laughed outright. "He really can't cook can he?"

"He can barbecue," Pearl said with a shrug as she finished folding the last of the few sweaters she had bought.

"Do you think...?" I began but stopped.

"What?" they all said in unison. It was comical. They were leaning towards me as though I was professing a secret.

"Oh nothing," I said with a wave of my hand and folding my legs up on Pearl's bed.

"Do we think that Merrick likes you?" Rayne asked her eyes wide with excitement.

"Oh no, not that," I said. "That might take some time. I guess I just wondered if you think I should wear different clothes, or maybe change my hair or something." My fingers pulled on my dry bob of strands.

"Well I think you shouldn't change anything," Rayne said. "Merrick likes you the way you are. He picked you after all." I was tempted to tell her why he had truly picked me, but bit my tongue.

"Although," Coral began, "he does like girls with long hair," she finished saying as she gently touched a lock of my hair. "Maybe you could grow it longer."

"Do you use conditioner?" Pearl asked me, hearing the rough scratch of my hair between Corals fingers.

"Yes," I said unable to hide my exasperation. "I've tried everything, conditioner, leave in oil treatments, de-frizzing spray, shine protection. You name it, I put it in here to see if it would work." I gestured towards my head.

Rayne laughed. "My hair was like that too, before I transitioned. Here try this," she said handing me a pink swirled bottle of Head and Shoulders.

"Oh no I couldn't take the shampoo you just bought Rayne."

"Please take it Anya, as a gift, we all wanted to bring you back something. I enchanted that bottle to make hair extra smooth and silky so it should work wonders for you. I got you this rocking headband too, so it's kind of fitting" It was a gingham pattern in cobalt blue, a cute bow affixed to one of the sides.

"Oh right!" Coral said digging into her bag, "I bought you lip gloss in va va voom red."

"And I got you black nail polish," Peal said with a wink, "you've got a bit of that Goth thing going for you."

"You guys," I said blushing, "you're way too nice to me! I didn't even bring you anything."

"You kept Merrick company, and he's not grumpy now. That's good enough for us!" Rayne said with a thankful sigh.

"Yes!" Coral and Pearl chimed in as well.

A soft rap at the door drew our attention to it and Ondine opened the door.

"I'm sorry to break up the fun girls, but it's getting late and I really should be getting Anya home."

Coral whined, "Awwww, pooper."

We all laughed, but I gathered my things, placing them in a small plastic bag that Pearl handed me, and thanked them again for the gifts. Rayne went to start up the van and Ondine turned to speak to me before joining her.

"Merrick is on the front porch Anya, if you would like to say goodbye to him. We'll be in the van waiting for you."

"Thank you," I said before she slipped out the side entrance. I made my way to the front porch and pulled on my boots. Sure enough, Merrick was seated there on the bench. He stood as I approached.

"What's in the bag?" he asked me and I opened it up for him to see. He reached down and pulled out the nail polish, as he examined it, he arched an eyebrow.

"Pearl bought it for me," I said with a smile. "I really like it."

"Black eh?" he asked, and I nodded.

"Wicked." He added, his voice throaty as he plopped it back into its place and looked back up to my eyes.

"Thanks for the great day, Merrick," I said rushing forward to give him a hug, my head sliding under his chin. I didn't even care if I wasn't being cool. I was way too happy to have friends who were so thoughtful. Being honest with myself, the night truly had been great. Were it not for this arranged meeting, I would have simply spent the night reading.

"No problem, Buttercup," he said as I backed away ready to leave.

I frowned. "Buttercup? Really?"

"I could call you, Petunia, instead." He said with a smirk.

"Really, Merrick, you've got to think of a more original nickname for me." I shook my head, but I was fighting back a smile and then waved before I walked to the van.

By the time I got home, I was exhausted and it was eleven o'clock. I was going to go straight to bed.

"How was your night?" my parents asked meeting me at the door.

"Great!" I said with a smile. "I'm beat and heading to bed."

"Wait! Don't we get any details, Anya?" My father called out to me as I walked up the stairs.

"Well, Merrick and I hung out in the shed for a bit while he fixed his bike. I made supper, which we both enjoyed and then we watched a documentary on sharks. All in all, it was pretty fun."

"That's it?" My mother asked.

"Yep," I replied. There was no way I was telling them he kissed me!

They both looked at one another and shrugged and with that I headed to my room and changed quickly, brushing my teeth, then collapsing into the covers.

Chapter 6

IT HAD BEEN TWO weeks since I had arrived in Seabright, and things were finally starting to fall into a routine. I had become closer to Leah and Evelyn, and really began to enjoy spending time with them. They were funny, and sarcastic, and incredibly intelligent. It was like we were kindred spirits. If I was late for lunch or arrived for a class after them they were worried, or wondered where I was.

Pearl and Rayne were just as close- like sisters to me really, and whenever I ran into them they kept suggesting that I should come over to their house sometime for a girl's night.

It was a strange feeling to have them all want me around. It was peculiar to me to feel wanted, to feel like I belonged.

I arrived at school and said goodbye to Rodney hopping down the stairs. My mother had helped me make invitations for a get together with my new friends. I hadn't really had sleepovers in my pre-teens, so it would be my first sort of birthday party or celebration.

Entering the main hall, I walked towards the lockers where I could usually find Rayne and Pearl. My eyes searched until they found them, and not far off was Merrick and a group of males, all clearly Mers. There were four of them altogether, and my senses lit up. It was a strange feeling something like being close to sand and ocean water.

I couldn't help but look at Merrick while I walked over, until a couple of girls walked up to him and his friends and my attention switched to them. Both of them were older than me. The first had long curly brown hair and green eyes, the second had auburn hair in long messy layers and blue eyes rimmed in eyeliner. The second sidled up to Merrick and placed her hand on his forearm, laughing at something he had said. Something about their conversation made me uneasy

"Hey Anya!" I heard Pearl say to me, pulling my eyes in her direction.

"Hey!" I said, still feeling slightly thrown.

Rayne nodded in the direction of the redhead. "Don't worry about Gina, she's got nothing on you."

They had seen me look at Merrick. I could feel my face grow warm with embarrassment.

Pearl groaned. "Ugh, she's the worst. I don't know why Merrick even bothers with her."

I shrugged and smiled, pretending to not care. Or did I really care? I couldn't tell. Honestly I hardly knew Merrick anyway; one night of hanging out clearly did not make us a couple, especially since we both agreed time would dictate how things went for us.

"I came over to talk with you ladies anyway," I said with a bright smile, "never mind boys." They both smiled at me.

Rayne winked at me and then whispered. "Yeah we know. My mom called your mom this morning. You're coming home with us after school. We can't make it to your birthday thing on the first of December since our father has some Mer military function. Your mom is dropping your stuff off at our house as we speak." She looked at Gina again now draped over Merrick and scowled.

Pearl moved in closer to me. "I would still love to have my invitation though. I've never gotten one for anything." I handed it to her and her hand smoothed over the envelope in admiration. "Oh it's so pretty."

It was a sea shell set of cards in shades of purple and blue that my mother had bought at a craft store. As a finishing touch, my mom had even showed me how to write with a calligraphy pen and ink. There was nothing Mers appreciated more than small trinkets of beauty.

"Coral was jumping around like a dolphin when she found out you were coming over tonight. Meet us here after school, kay?" Rayne added. Then her voice darkened, "Ugh, sometimes I want to box Merrick's ears. WHAT'S HE THINKING?"

That was loud enough to get the attention of Merrick, Gina and everyone surrounding them. Pearl, for the first time I had ever witnessed, looked smug and Rayne's eyes looked stormy as they centred on Gina. My eyes grew wide with surprise and I scratched my head lightly while turning in the opposite direction and averting the gaze of the group.

"Who is that ugly uni-brow girl with your sisters

Merrick?" I heard a voice ask loudly, and I turned back around slowly to see Gina's blue eyes scanning over me.

UGLY?! I knew I was no Mer, but she didn't have to insult me!

I had the feeling that I was not going to like this Gina person one bit, but I didn't react.

Merrick sighed, a heavy one that didn't sound very pleasing at all. Only, I couldn't tell if the sigh was because he was considering how to explain who I was to this girl, who clearly liked him, or whether it was the question that made him annoyed.

"She's a friend of the family Gina, that's all. Just don't worry about it."

I couldn't help but feel a little wounded, especially when Rayne and Pearl gave me sympathetic looks. I shrugged it off. Nothing was going to stop me from being excited about my first ever—girl's night. Then I really smiled, tonight would be filled with fun. The bell rang, it's ringing chime giving me an annoying jolt.

"I'll see you guys later!" I said to Rayne and Pearl and briskly walked passed Merrick and Gina.

"What does she mean she'll see your sister's later?" Gina asked. Only this time I didn't wait around to hear Merrick's weak excuse.

CLASSES SEEMED TO FLY BY. I think it had to do with the fact that I was eager for the day to be done. Before I knew it, I was waiting by the lockers for Rayne and Pearl. They came bolting towards me with stricken expressions on their faces, speaking to me rapidly. I didn't catch much of anything until they slowed down, their breaths steadying.

"Whatever happens, just say no," Rayne said.

"Or you could pretend that you can't hear."

Pearl nodded and then added. "Don't make any sudden movements- she's like a snake."

I watched them, amused while they uttered their absurdities. When they stopped abruptly, looking down the hall, I could see why. Gina was walking alongside Merrick and heading in our direction.

They caught up with us and Rayne and Pearl crossed their arms in disapproval.

"Hey ladies," Gina said to them with a smile, and I noticed her unease with them. She looked as though she wanted their approval, but could tell she didn't have any sympathy. "So Merrick tells me you are all celebrating Anna's birthday tonight. Can I come?"

"ANYA, and no you may not." Rayne corrected her, and a smile pulled up from the corner of my mouth. For some reason I wasn't angry anymore just amused by Gina; this close I could actually examine her. She was taller than me and a bit shorter than Merrick, but not nearly as pretty as Rayne or Pearl. She wore too much makeup to try and fill the gap, but her skin looked dull. She was slim, not curvy like a Mer and even her blue eyes were devoid of vivid colour. She looked sad, pathetic almost. I wondered if Merrick kissed her the way he had kissed me, if it was her supposed sexiness that appealed to him.

Merrick had watched me gauge her. She looked at him in a pleading sort of way and nudged his arm.

"Why don't you let Anya decide Rayne? It is her birthday thing." Merrick said, looking at me with a challenging gleam.

And then everyone was looking at me. I didn't

falter. I had already known what I would say. I wondered if he thought this were some type of game between the two of us to see who would cave first and beg the other to try and date. He had told me what he wanted; time to be young- and clearly stupid- so I would give it to him.

"I don't mind you coming Gina, but it's not my house, or my car, so that part you'll have to settle with Rayne and Pearl."

They both seemed shocked with my response, so I sent out an emotive wave letting them know my reasoning. If anything confirmed to me that I was indeed a Mer, it was my uncanny empathic abilities. Merrick caught a whiff of it too because his eyes went straight to me in awe.

I had let Rayne and Pearl know that I felt sorry for Gina, clearly she felt she had something to prove and I had the benefit of their friendship while she didn't, which was something I was grateful for and gave me advantage. I felt much stronger than her. They smiled at me.

"Fine," Rayne said at last, "but after we pick up Coral, Anya will have to sit with Merrick in the front."

"Oh no I can," Gina said trying to regain control of the situation, which was hard to do with Rayne around, "it's no big deal."

"You're too big," Pearl said, all of a sudden finding her voice in the situation. "Anya is clearly the smallest so it makes sense for her to sit with Merrick."

Gina cast Merrick an accusatory glance, probably since he said nothing to defend her.

"That's dangerous," she said quickly.

"You're the one who invited yourself over, otherwise there would be plenty room," Rayne added gesturing towards the doors, "let's get going already."

We all piled into the car and when we reached Coral's school she came squealing over, her curls bouncing with each step. Luckily by the time we got there, the school had been emptied and no one else was loitering.

When she opened the door she didn't hide her disdain. "What's she doing here?" She mumbled quietly. I tried to distract her from Gina's presence.

"Hey Coral," I said with a smile, "I'm going to hop in the front, just give me one second." I unbuckled my seat belt and stepped out of the car.

"Anya it's so nice to see you!" Coral said pulling me into a hug that I returned happily. It was sad that I was a year older than Coral, but still she looked more like a Mermaid than me.

Merrick opened the door and adjusted the seat so that it was pushed as far back as it could go. "Do you have leg space Coral?" He asked while looking at me and gesturing for me to sit in his lap.

"Yep." Coral replied.

We ended up positioned so that I sat in between Merrick's legs and leaned back against his chest. Gina sent me icy cold looks while Merrick's attention was diverted. He buckled us in, and subtly touched the window making it frost over. Even though what I was doing was strangely reckless and unlike me, I felt safe pressed against Merrick, and incredibly warm. His breaths fell even on my neck and he ended up wrapping both arms around me so that he could sit comfortably.

It felt like we were soul bound, and reminded me of old paintings I had seen in my father's historical books. Mer's wrapped around one another for portraits, such peculiar creatures with their overwhelming love bonds. I wanted to nuzzle against his neck and cheek and I think he started to feel the same connected emotions too, because his hand pressed against my stomach and pulled me closer. It had to do with the contract our parents signed for our pairing. Contracts of that sort always had a magical bond woven within. Something that deep seated was hard to resist, especially in close quarters.

    I could see Gina watching whatever she could in the rear-view mirror, but I had no sympathy for her. She had been unkind to me, and she had no idea who we all were. She didn't even know that Merrick and I were bound. I thought about the romantic supper we had shared, and the kisses he had planted on my lips. For a few seconds I luxuriated in the feeling of his embrace. It was nice, until I recalled his desire for more time, and reaffirmed to myself that it was only one night of many to come much later on in our lives. I straightened and pulled my body forward, only to have him pull me back. He clench his thighs around mine. His nose brushed my neck inconspicuously to catch the scent of my perfume. Looking in the rear-view mirror I could see there was possession in his eyes, and I knew Gina saw it too. So I pinched him, the underside of his arm, away from view so that he would snap out of our bonding enchantment. The jerky reaction his hand made told me I was successful, and he whispered his thanks.

    Rayne looked at us smugly as if she had proved something to us both by smooshing us together in the front of their car. Her eyes were mischievous and suddenly her mouth was smiling in amusement. Pearl and Coral joined her with their own smiles, clearly able to pick up on the emotions we were emitting so intensely.

Chapter 7

WHEN WE ALL PILED out of the car Gina looked displeased. I had expected her to be sad or angry, but instead she latched onto Merrick's hand and seemed to hold on for dear life.

"I'm glad I finally get to meet your parents Merrick." She said smiling almost sweetly, and again I felt pity for her.

"They're not here," Coral responded immediately, while we all walked towards the door.

"Oh. They're not?" Gina asked, looking up at Merrick with a worried expression.

"No," he said, "They're working in Halifax tonight, but they'll be back later."

I guess I wasn't the only one whose parents had to work long hours in the Mer community. It made me wonder what project was so important that it was keeping all of our parents so preoccupied. The past few years, my parents had been needed more and more by the Mecrutia Council and High Order. I had assumed that it was only because I had grown older that they agreed to do the extra work, but now I was starting to wonder.

"Where's Zale?" I asked suddenly remembering that the Prices had a younger brother, one I had initially mistaken for my future husband.

"Zale was accepted to a school for the gifted, near our parents work, so he gets a drive with them every morning." Rayne looked at me speaking slowly enough so that I could tell her words were chosen carefully. She was suggesting that I read between the lines, which I did.

Zale was a *Sealatian,* a chosen one from our Mers to attend their schooling on the base camp where our parents would work. It was an opportunity given to those who excel in specific Mer capabilities from an early age. Water manipulation, enchantment, and empathy were common gifts they wanted to cultivate and strengthen. It was rare among Mers to have the opportunity to attend Sealatia Ceremonies.

I had been offered a chance to join when I was eleven because of my empathy, but had declined. There was something strangely cold about the teachers that made me feel uncomfortable. At first my father suggested that perhaps it was simply because I could not read them as well as other Mers, but I felt that it was something more akin to fear. The Sealatia made me fearful, because there was no humanity in them, and I could tell instantly that they had disliked the human in me. We had once been humans though, all Mers had, long long ago and so that kind of prejudice didn't make sense to me.

"Oh," I said in response, sending a wave of

emotion to Rayne, letting her know that I had understood what she had meant to say through omission. I wondered what Zale's gift was, and I wondered why he seemed so incredibly warm and adorable when I had met him. Other *Sealatia* seemed so calculated and exacting.

"Who's Zale?" Gina asked.

"Our brother," Rayne snapped back.

"I am so hungry I could eat a whole swordfish!" Coral exclaimed with an exasperated groan.

"Me too," Pearl added, "only I think I want catfish instead with potatoes and—"

"I wanted to have the trout tonight," Merrick interrupted.

"We're having salmon." Rayne said ending the debate there. "I took the salmon out this morning and seasoned it while all you lazy buggers were still sleeping."

"You sure like your fish," Gina said looking up at Merrick with a twinkle in her eye.

"You have no idea," Merrick whispered under his breath.

I smiled at him, enjoying the resonance to his voice. There was something compelling about it each time he spoke that made me want to draw closer to him. Gina watched me, and I turned my face quickly, my eyes bulging in personal punishment for being so obvious in my attraction to Merrick. Maybe, even I was still feeling the effects of the car ride.

Gina and Merrick planted themselves in the living room on the couch while she insisted they watch one of Pearl's romantic comedies. I felt sorry for him, but then maybe he liked the fact that she was feminine and demanding. I knew that I sure as shells wasn't.

"ANYA WOULD YOU HELP US MAKE A SAUCE LIKE THE ONE YOU MADE FOR MERRICK LAST WEEKEND?" Coral asked me across the kitchen island.

Merrick's ears pricked up, but luckily Gina didn't seem to hear because she was too busy ranting about Stacey something or other.

"Shhhh," I said my eyes large, before I winked. "Coral, you're being a troublemaker. Your poor brother wants to be a normal boy." I was poking fun, but really I had understood what he wanted. Only, I desperately wanted to be what he was running away from.

Coral burst out laughing and Rayne and Pearl giggled wickedly while they cut potatoes.

Gina's phone rang and suddenly she was ranting even more vehemently to the person on the other line.

"So much for celebrating with us," I said.

"Thank Poseidon!" Pearl said.

It was nice that we were all doing our part to make supper. It meant that in no time the food would be done, and I was starting to get hungry. I was busy working away on cutting onions, when a really pungent one wafted up and my eyes began to tear, drops running down my cheeks. It was my least favourite thing about cooking with onions, even though I loved them.

"What mischief are you Mers up to?" Merrick asked from behind me.

"Nothing," Coral replied coyly turning from her own cutting to look at us both by the kitchen island. She gestured for me to turn and face him, but I hesitated. When I turned to look at him, his eyes went all soft and gooey-like. He immediately cupped my face with both palms and wiped away my tears with his thumbs.

"Why are you crying?" he asked his voice sweet. My mouth opened and I wished I had some sort of witty remark to spit out, but I was at a loss for words with those deep teal eyes fixated on my face.

"Onions," I finally whispered after almost a minute of intense gazing at one another. He looked behind me to see them on the cutting board and then nodded.

"Oh good. Makes sense," he said curtly. Then backed up awkwardly, after he had reached over my shoulder to grab an apple.

"Aren't you going to grab Gina one, Merrick?" Rayne asked in a teasing tone.

"She doesn't like fruit," he said and walked back to the living room. Gina's voice was finally calming as she was finished talking on her phone.

When I turned back around, Coral was leaning on the kitchen island with her chin nestled in her hands. She was looking at me wistfully. Pearl had her hand clutched against her heart and both sighed.

"I know that's my brother and all, but I wish my mate was that sweet with me, and wiped away my tears. We never have moments like that- Murdock is such an ass," Coral said.

Pearl nodded. "I agree. Mine is too far away for us to bond like that right now, but when he's here, he is wonderful."

"We weren't bonding," I said in protest, finishing the onions and moving onto the tomato.

"All of you have mates already?" I asked trying to divert the attention from me. Of course they did, they were beautiful and *looked* like Mers.

"That Mer in the car with us a couple of weeks ago is my mate. You must see him at school with

Merrick sometimes. Murdock." Coral said spitting out his name bitterly.

"He's an ass?" I asked, wondering how on earth she would have chosen a poor mate. Coral was so fun and vibrant.

"He's just a little serious, and well a bit of a bad boy right now," Rayne added.

"We're all hoping he grows out of it," Pearl said.

"Yeah for my sake," Coral added. "I agreed to him because I thought it would make my parents happy, but now I wish I had waited like Merrick. I don't even know why he picked me," she huffed. "He just isn't romantic at all. He gets so irritated with me sometimes- especially when I'm cheerful!"

"That doesn't sound nice," I said trying to be careful with my words. "You should tell him when he's being a jerk."

"I know," Coral said, "but I'm too nice, and he's so bossy."

"You'll find your own way to put him in his place," I said with a wink. "You're too strong a Mer not to."

Coral perked up at my words. "You really think so?"

"I know so," I said. "I can feel it."

"Yeah, that is amazing what you can do," Rayne began, "those empathic waves are incredible."

"Thanks!" I gushed.

Pearl sighed again.

"You miss him?" I asked already knowing that she did.

"Yeah," she said, "His name is Merlin. We spend a lot of time together in the summers when he's visiting his uncle Arturo. This year he went to Military training college in the mid-Atlantic, though."

"Merlin!" I said, "Your mate is Merley?" I couldn't contain my excitement even though I tried not to raise my voice to hearing level for Gina. Although she seemed pretty clueless, I couldn't be careless.

I had met Merlin a few years ago when Arturo had brought him on one of his visits to meet with my parents. He was one of the kindest Mers I had ever met, and someone I considered family, a good friend. Not to mention he was absolutely stunning. At seventeen now, he was gorgeous. His eyes were sea green, and his skin had a bronze complexion from his Spanish mother and Malagasy father. He was soft spoken and intelligent, but an incredibly skilled warrior from a long line of science Mers. His warrior skills were unusual for a family such as his, but much like my mother, a science Mer from a long line of warriors, he pursued his dream despite his family's discouraging words.

"You know him?" Pearl asked excitedly.

"He's like my cousin," I said proudly. "I call Arturo my uncle even though there's no blood relation."

"By Poseidon, Merlin is one dreamy Mer," Coral said with a sigh. "I wish Murdock was that gorgeous.

"Murdock is cute," I said remembering his curly blonde hair and light grey eyes.

"Meh," Coral replied with a shrug.

Rayne smiled. "Even I agree with you on that one Anya, and you all know what my mate looks like. Actually, I haven't even showed you a picture yet have I?" She went to her purse left on one of the kitchen stools. Pulling out the photo, she did it with such care that I could tell just how much she felt for him.

"His name is River," she said handing me a picture of him in his navy warrior fatigues. His hair was pitch black and fell just above his shoulders, it was streaked with purple on his front bangs, and he was clearly in his early twenties. His eyes were violet and a broad and white smile drew my eyes in instantly. No wonder Rayne had changed her hair.

"River and Rayne…" She whispered softly. "He dyes his hair black, he's so silly. It looks like this naturally." She showed me another picture of a blonde River, still striking and handsome.

"Wow," was all I could manage before I added, "he's a hunk."

Rayne actually giggled. It seemed so unlike her and I could tell that River was definitely her weak spot.

"Isn't he?" Pearl said fanning herself.

Coral pouted. "Totally wish Murdock was yummier."

"Oh my gosh, we're bad," I said suddenly realizing that most of our conversation had been about guys.

"You think this is bad?" Rayne started, "wait until the first time you go into heat. Oh boy that's an ordeal on its own. The last time River did, he stole away from his training camp, in the southern Atlantic Ocean, just so he could come see me."

My eyes started to sparkle mischievous and I wrinkled my nose a bit, wondering if Merrick would ever do the same for me. "That's adorable though."

Rayne laughed outright. "Yeah it was, but he was in SO much trouble. Apparently he had to tell his commanding officer he was in heat. Even then, he was in for punishment big time, until one of his friends said that River should show the commanding officer my picture. After which -for some reason- he gave him pardon."

"Well, you *are* beautiful," I said in earnest. "All of you are."

"Every Mer is," Pearl said.

"Not every," I replied twisting my mouth.

"Oh Anya," Coral started, "you're beautiful too, and before you know it you'll transcend with the rest of us."

Pearl came over and hugged me in comfort. Rayne nodded her head in agreement vehemently before speaking. "You're gonna knock the socks off of Merrick."

"You gals are the best friends a Mer could have." I replied letting myself relax. They were right about one thing, eventually I would *have* to transcend.

"You think that's the best...Pearl show her." Rayne looked over at her sister in encouragement.

"No I don't think—"

"Do it!" Coral said energetically.

"Okay, watch this," Pearl said as a trickle of water from a nearby glass, slowly crawled up, like a snake in a barrel and swirled upward into the pattern of a Victorian star. Each point was swirling and shifting three dimensionally. It was tiny, no larger than the end of a tablespoon, but it was incredible.

"Albayraous" She spoke enchanting the star.

"It's a beauty star!" I said with a gasp.

Pearl smiled, "yes, *but* it only shows the bearer of the spell their true beauty, it doesn't create what is not already present in the person."

"How do I use it?" I asked in awe watching the star float down to levitate above my open palm. Now fully formed and spinning concentrically it was changing colours.

"It'll heat up in a minute. Then it will evaporate and for five to ten minutes you'll be able to see yourself as you would with your true beauty manifested."

I was mesmerized by the shape, and it began to mist. My heart hammered a little faster in anticipation.

"What are you guys doing?" Gina asked behind me. My heart nearly jumped into my throat at the sound of her voice.

"Nothing!" Coral said and I shifted to block the star. It was almost completely gone but there was no way I would be able to capture the mist with Gina standing there. She would see the change in me immediately.

"Well, what are you guys making?" Gina asked.

"Fish, brussel sprouts, and perogies," Pearl offered as an answer while Rayne walked next to me and leaned back on the island to block the star from the other side.

"I don't really like fish," Gina said. "Don't you guys have anything else?"

"Not really," Rayne said, starting to look annoyed. "The food will be done in about twenty minutes anyway."

"Is there anything to snack on then?" Gina asked. In my eyes she was pushing her luck, but I guessed she must have felt hungry.

Pearl and Coral both gestured to the fruit bowl, and Rayne matched them by pointing her knife there as well.

"Nevermind," Gina huffed and left the room, thankfully not asking any more questions. We were all relieved.

Her parents called her before the food was even finished, furious that she had not told them where she was going after school, but she didn't seem to care. Fifteen minutes later, when her dad showed up to pick her up, he looked disapprovingly at Rayne for not ensuring that she had called them. Gina didn't take any responsibility, and her father, Mr. Amos, threatened to have a word with their parents. He was giving Merrick unfavourable looks when Rayne apologized, which I knew killed her a little on the inside. So, I stepped up to take the blame and tried to smooth things out.

"Mr. Amos, it's really my fault. See, it's my birthday next weekend and I invited Gina to come along with us. We got so distracted in the kitchen, since we were all hungry, that we didn't make note of the time."

His stern exterior started to soften, until he glanced at Merrick. Gina had no sense to let go of his arm, and was still wrapped around him. Even though I kind of wanted Gina's father to disliked my mate, it would be selfish of me. I sent out a calming wave of emotion.

"Please don't be too angry with Gina for my excitement." I added an inflection I so rarely used, my honeyed words, drenched in empathic energy, reached out to him. Then, his emotions unravelled, and he was like putty.

"I'm sorry, girls. It's okay. I understand, but Gina, you're coming home with me. Your mother wants to speak with you." I smiled at him softly though my eyes were still intense.

"Have a wonderful evening..." He looked embarrassed that he didn't know my name.

"Anya," I supplied him, the same emotional evocation in my words. At least I could plant fondness in his heart, so that if Gina were to speak poorly of me, he would doubt it at first.

"Well I hope you have a wonderful birthday celebration, Anya," Mr. Amos said before he made a 'come here' gesture to Gina. She pouted and stomped her foot like a child, but gathered her things and followed. As soon as the door closed, everyone but Merrick, let out a sigh of relief.

Rayne rushed forward and hugged me. "Anya you were awesome! Thank you for saving me." Pearl and Coral agreed, but when I turned around to Merrick he had a dark look on his face.

"Why did you do that?" He asked me.

"We'll give you two a moment," Rayne and pushed Coral and Pearl along. I nodded to them before answering.

"What do you mean?" I asked. *Shouldn't you be grateful?* I wanted to say. He could continue on with his life plan of freedom.

"You took the blame. You used your powers to smooth things out for me."

"Not just you!" I snapped raising my chin a little, "Rayne didn't deserve the blame for your girlfriend's actions." I couldn't help it, and I spit out the last part with a bit of edge that I tried too late to soften.

"My girlfriend?" He said challenging me, still angry that I had interfered.

I shrugged. I wanted to roll my eyes, but that would just create more distance between us and he had already asked me to be understanding.

Then, I did the only think that seemed natural. I sent a wave of comfort to him. It was meant to be tender and soothing and was dripping with affection. I watched his face as it cascaded over him, and noticed a visible tug in him when it reached the pit of his stomach.

"I'm giving you what you want, Merrick. You could at least be thankful." The words were not inflected as seriously as they had been with Mr. Amos, just enough to take the edge off of our emotions. I suspected he was only angry with me because I made him feel guilty. I did what he could not.

He closed his eyes. "Thank you." He managed to say before opening them. That was when I truly saw what was making him angry. His eyes were filled with fear, and affection, and I didn't know what had triggered the cause of either. *Did he fear me and my power?* He shouldn't, he knew I had never used it on him until that moment. And the affection intermixed was unexpected, but so strongly evident.

"Promise me you won't use that power over me again Anya." It was a command and a plea.

"Okay," I said letting the power release from me so my words were neutral.

"And don't fight my battles for me."

"I'm your mate. I'm supposed to protect you."

"I'm supposed to protect *you*, Anya."

"Whatever. Again Merrick, not everything I did was for you tonight. Now let's go eat, I'm starving."

"You're impossible."

"Look, I promised I wouldn't use my powers on you again. I'm giving you your space. What more do you want?" By then I was frustrated and beginning to get cranky. I was hungry and he was keeping me from my supper.

"You don't understand Anya."

"Understand what!?" My hands jerked out.

"You get irritated when you're hungry?" He said, realizing there was more in my words than simply submission to his request.

"Yes," I replied exasperated. "My stomach is eating itself."

We both looked down towards it and he laughed. It felt --unexpected.

"What on earth are you going to be like when you're pregnant with our Mer babies?"

I had not expected him to say anything remotely similar to those words and it was worse than seeing Gina latched onto his arms. I wanted to ask him to stop saying things like that, to stop being sweet to me when I least expected it, and to never speak of our future again, but Coral came prancing into the room.

"Your food is getting cold guys."

I tore my eyes from him, though it felt more painful than tearing a strip of skin off of my body and followed her. I wanted to run into his arms and kiss him. I wanted to tell him that I didn't agree to him dating other people because he was mine, but I couldn't. My pride wouldn't let me, and my heart wasn't so sure yet. Magic had a way of warping things.

Chapter 8

FOR THE REST OF the night I hid out in Pearl's room with the Price girls. Mr. and Mrs. Price had returned from their day of work with Zale, and all three were happy that a delicious supper was waiting for them. They complimented me for my subtle spice suggestions, which seemed to make the meal more enjoyable for them than usual.

I couldn't bring myself to be near Merrick, even when Rayne asked if I wanted to spend some time with him before we got all girlish. I declined, and we watched a few episodes of a show called H2O, funnily about Mermaids.

"Do you want us to grab you a glass of juice or anything while we're down in the kitchen?" Coral asked. They were heading to get some snacks, but I was full still from dessert. I had already gone to fill my glass with water.

"Nope!" I answered, grabbing my oversized t-shirt, tooth brush, and toothpaste. I hummed walking to the bathroom, and closed the door to change. After I brushed my teeth, I took a look in the mirror. For the most part I avoided looking into them, but lately, more and more often, I would catch a glimpse of myself in one, and suddenly experience an emotional plummet. This time, I hadn't gotten that far. I jumped when I heard a knock at the door.

Merrick spoke through, "are you done in there pipsqueak?" I grimaced at the nickname and picked up my pile of folded clothes, my things were set neatly atop. I whipped open the door, and gave him a sharp look.

"Stop calling me that, and yes, it's all yours!" I was annoyed, but the emotion quickly melted and morphed to shyness when I realized he wasn't wearing a shirt. Blocking the entryway, he was leaning in the door frame, his lower half, thankfully covered in red plaid flannel pyjama pants. He was biting a nail, nonchalant, and straightened walking into the bathroom. I took a few steps back evading him, and he closed the door locking us both in, which had me feeling a little claustrophobic. I was almost in panic mode, especially when I actually raised my averted eyes from the floor to look into this eyes. I was starting to realize just how roguish Merrick was.

"Well I should leave you to it," I started trying to move around him, but he blocked me while still brushing his teeth.

"Merrick!" I said frustrated but trying to keep the volume to a minimum. I didn't want his parents to stumble across the two of us in the bathroom together. Actually, I didn't want anyone to know we were in there together. It was risky, and my heart was hammering faster than a jackhammer. I pulled down on my t-shirt nightie, which suddenly didn't seem long enough. He finally finished brushing his teeth and checked them in the mirror, placing the toothbrush back into the holder. He turned to face me and I crossed my arms.

"What do you want?" I asked.

"Nothing." He said, but I waited for him to say more. "Are you mad at me, little mouse?"

I groaned, but didn't reply. I refused to let him think he could call me that nickname.

His sockless feet inched forward, and his toes tickled mine. "Huh Anya? Are you mad at me?" I pulled my foot back. He was playing with me, but I was still annoyed from his berating nicknames.

"You are," he said closing the distance but I stood my ground. "You're mad at me. That's why you're not talking to me. Well, I'll have to fix that."

Something in his eyes shifted, and his hands shot forward and started poking me and I jumped back trying to avoid him. Before I knew it I was breathless and giggling.

"Merrick stop! Stop!" I pleaded.

"Say mercy," he said still jabbing at me while his eyes gleamed.

He had me backed against the towel rack in the wall with one more step back, it would hurt.

"Mercy!" I cried out.

"Good," he said "I grant your mercy. Now give me a goodnight kiss."

My giggles stopped immediately from pure shock. He leaned down so that his lips were inches from mine, but they hovered there. *Was he going to kiss me again?* Maybe he did like me more than I thought. I froze, unable to move, and he noticed the change in my demeanour.

"I was just joking, Anya" he said, his voice rich and teasing my lips. A loud knock on the door had us both turning our heads.

"Hurry up in there!" Zale cried. "I've got to go! I drank a litre of juice." His voice was clearly audible through the door and I was afraid it would call attention to the whole house. Merrick swung open the door, and gave Zale a glaring look before brushing past him.

I followed quickly, but Zale stopped me. "Wait Anya."

I turned to look at him. He was adorable, leaning in the doorway similarly to Merrick. Only he wore a blue tee and pyjama pants, his blonde hair falling into his eyes.

"You okay?" I asked noticing the darkening change in his face. He looked tormented and tired. I felt an indescribable kinship to him in that moment, and the word *brother,* echoed in my mind. He glanced back at Merrick's closed bedroom door.

"I will be okay." He said to me. His words held weight to them and I suddenly had the urge to open up to him emotionally. I shifted into my powers slowly, and felt an oncoming rush of his sadness and anger. I wondered if it had to do with being a Sealatian and suddenly I worried for him. There was a dark cloud of emotion close to his heart. So I reached out to him, and placed my hand on his shoulder in comfort.

"Whatever it is Zale that's bothering you, I'm sure things will work out. It'll be okay." Then I reached out to him emotionally and took away his heavy feelings, replacing them with something light and comforting. He softened and I watched his shoulders relax, as though some menacing darkness had been removed from whispering behind him. His eyes intensified, looking at me as though he was at ease. His face seemed moonlight before he spoke again.

"You are everything I thought you would be." It was a soft whisper off his tongue, like he was chanting a spell. His hand had moved over mine and rested there in comfort. Yet, the words he spoke made me wonder. *What did he mean by that?* Why would he wonder about me, and did this have to do with me being a potential Sealatian. *Had the girls mentioned my powers to Zale?*

"Zale?" I asked, hoping he would elaborate. He didn't though, he just placed his free hand against my cheek.

"Will you help me Anya?"

I had no idea what he was asking of me, yet I felt compelled to say yes. I could not resist the swallowing depths of his blue eyes, so brightened and like shining orbs. *Was he manipulating me with his powers?* I wondered briefly before the thought drifted away like a log caught in a wave.

"Yes." I said. "I will help you."

He broke our touch and the moment dissipated to an awkward hallway encounter.

"Thank you," he said. "You are the *one*."

He repeated himself and I nodded not knowing what else to say. He disappeared into the bathroom closing the door. I turned away from him, feeling bereft and as though I was on autopilot. I found my way back to Pearl's room on the second floor.

When I sat with the girls, all gathered in front of the television with pillows and bean bag chairs, immediately I felt lightened. Yet, the intense encounter with their younger brother was still weighing on my mind. *What had he meant by saying I was the one? And why did he need my help?*

Had I been tactless at that given time, like my usual self, I would have simply asked them all what powers Zale had. I thought it might be best to wait for a later time, though, when my question wouldn't be followed with an inquisition as to why I had asked.

My thoughts were quickly replaced with laughs as we talked and painted each other's nails. One of the bottles of nail polish remover was knocked over when Coral bounced by, and Pearl quickly held her hand out stopping the liquid from spilling over, and making it levitate. Coral fixed the bottle upright and slowly Pearl directed the liquid back into the container. It made sense that she had water manipulation like Merrick, the two were twins.

Coral giggled as she watched. "I wish I could do that too," she said with a sigh. "Or control the weather and speak to water animals like Rayne."

"I can only control it in a close area," Rayne said to better explain her powers.

"What are your powers Coral?" I asked.

"I have healing powers." She said and pouted.

"The most useful powers out of the three of us, and she complains," Rayne said with a smirk.

I laughed, and nestled into my pillow as Pearl turned off the lights and Rayne played the next episode for us to watch.

Sometime later, curled up in my sleeping bag on a futon, with many layers of blankets beneath me, darkness crept in, and I slept.

Chapter 9

FOR MY COMPLETE DISLIKE of school as an institution, I did happen to thoroughly enjoy my English classes, and had been looking forward to my afternoon English class since that morning. It also helped that since the beginning of the term we had been completing reading circles. We chose a book to read from a selected list, and then met daily with the same group to discuss our progress and our thoughts about what we had read.

There was a boy in my group named, Seth, who I had grown quite fond of, and was looking forward to seeing every class. It was more than just his cute face, it felt like we had meaningful conversations when we spoke, and he was thoughtful and intelligent. There weren't many boys I had befriended, but I felt like he could be a true friend. He raised literary points and encouraged discussion that I found incredibly interesting, especially since he was so passionate about the literature.

Sometimes in the past I had found this off putting in my peers. Some of them were so competitive, too eager to prove themselves, but he was so charismatic that it was endearing. Especially since when he looked at me his expressions never dimmed, he continued to be remarkable and enthusiastic.

For that very reason, and Gina's ugly unibrow girl comment, I had finally allowed my mother to show me how to groom my brows. It turned out far less painful than I had initially thought, and when I looked at myself in the mirror, it was as if my entire face had been changed. I now saw myself in a new light, and felt that once my braces were off in a few weeks, I might actually look a little cute.

Yet, despite that glimmer of hope, Monday had arrived and the start of the week brought a foreboding feeling of revenge. Gina had it out for me, but I had managed to evade her all morning. I knew why, but she searched for me like the plague, according to Leah there was nothing worse than inciting the wrath of the G-dog. Evelyn and Leah had given her the misnomer one day when Gina had shown up fir school in her usual mini-skirt and tank top beneath a hoodie combo, only that with it she had five layers of chain necklaces- one with a big pendant that said 'delicious'. The image was atrocious, but I could picture her walking down the halls looking down upon the minions with her oversized jewels.

She was looking for me now. That much I knew by word of Leah and Evie. It was lunch time, and I had avoided every hallway I knew she and the Mers used, to make my way to the cafeteria. I scolded myself for not bringing something to eat with me, but then I hadn't expected the grade ten queen bee to mark me as her next target. I glanced to where Evie and Leah usually sat. They were waiting for me and waved.

Quickly, I ordered a grilled cheese sandwich and grabbed an ice tea, paying and then placing everything on my tray. I was in the clear… or so I thought until I turned around and my jaw nearly dropped because Gina and her posse were seated at the first table in the row, the table I would have to pass to get to mine. They didn't even like coming to the cafeteria. She was seated on the table rather than a seat and was looking straight at me.

Merrick was noticeably absent, but Murdock was there, as well as Kai and Hurley. I cringed inwardly. I hadn't spoken much too the others, but I already knew that Murdock was not a fan of mine. He had been rude to me several times in our home period, which luckily he skipped half of the time, and was our only class together. Kai and Hurley seemed impartial, though I could tell they were surprised after they realized that I was Merrick's betrothed. There wasn't much I could do in response to their disapproval. I felt like a coward and walked really slowly with my tray. Would she try to trip me or something, luckily I hadn't left my iced tea open.

"Hey Anna," she said stopping me from walking by the table by jumping in front of me. "I had a lot of fun last week with you at Merrick's house."

She waited for my response. "Great," I replied, not knowing what else to say. I wanted to walk around her, but instead she leaned in closer.

"Listen," she began in a whisper, "you don't have to worry, your secrets safe with me."

"Secret?" I asked stupidly, dreading her

response.

Her volume returned. "You know, that you wet the bed." Everyone in the cafeteria grew silent.

My eyes darkened pinching together in a piercing gaze, but my voice was calm. "I don't do that, so you might want to check your sources G-dog. Especially since you left at six-thirty when your dad came to get you." And then I walked around her brushing her aside.

"What did you call me?" Her sharp voice was like a spear into the back.

I hadn't realized what I had called her until that moment, and I heard a shrill harpy cry behind me before my head was drenched in lukewarm coffee, spilling all over my sweater. I turned around to face my tormentor, who actually looked pretty pathetic with her stare of seething hatred.

"Oops," she said. "I slipped." Her pale blue eyes rolled and her long auburn hair was twined in her fingers. I wiped the coffee from face pushing back my hair and I squirmed as it dripped down my back. Merrick, like a phantom, appeared behind her.

"What happened?" he asked, his words directed at Gina, but he was clearly looking at me. His face was blank, trying to decipher the situation. It wouldn't take much imagination to figure out what had gone on.

"Nothing," I said before she even opened her mouth. "She tripped."

"I.. I..." she stammered, then looked at me in awe, probably wondering why on earth I might cover up her heinous move.

Merrick continued looking passively at me, but I could tell when his jaw ticked slightly that he wasn't convinced by my explanation. He looked over to his friends, anger in his eyes, but Kai and Hurley shrugged knowing, that Merrick wouldn't be happy if he knew they played along with Gina's scheme.

"Blech." I said shaking off some of the coffee. "Catch you later G-dog." I couldn't resist the last jab and then began the awkward walk to the bathroom. I wasn't going to wait around during Merrick's inquisition. As I walked, I wish that I had the power of water manipulation. At least then I could bead the coffee and stop it from soaking into my clothes.

No one had laughed at me, instead they seemed to be mortified by Gina's actions and probably by my cheeky follow up to her childish act. I might have looked like an eleven year old, but I wasn't about to start acting like one.

I found my way to the bathroom and before ducking my head beneath the water stream, I rinsed the sink out to clear the debris. I massaged quickly so that I would be able to get the sticky coffee feeling off of me. Tears streamed down my face, but the water took them away as soon as they were spilled. I couldn't help but feel emotional, confrontation always left me a little disheartened, but still I knew I had been victorious. I was joined a few minutes later by Evie and Leah.

"Oh my gosh you were A-MA-zing!" Evie cried out in her sing-song way.

Leah chortled reddening to the same colour as her hair. Until at last she caught her breath. "I cannot believe you called her G-dog,"

"Yeah, I wasn't going to be her victim," I said to them, but then pulled at my drenched sweater. "Ugh, I don't have anything else to wear."

"I have a t-shirt," Leah said gleeful, and pulled out a black, oversized t-shirt, which had the words wetlands scrawled across the front in green. "I use it for my environmental science work after school, but today it got cancelled. We don't need to do water chemistry lab until later."

It looked more like a tunic dress on me since Leah was taller, but it was far better than a wet sweater. At least I had English and Art class in the afternoon- a lighter half of the day -so I could relax a bit more. The rooms that the classes were held in were usually boiling as they were on the third floor. I considered myself lucky Gina picked today to seek revenge and not the day I had Math for last class when I'd be stuck in the freezing west corridor.

I made a mental note to keep a spare change of clothes in my locker from now on. If I was going to be at this high school for the next two years with Gina, I might need them. I pulled out my emergency kit and used the comb in it to brush back my wet hair and decided to finally use the va va voom lip gloss Coral had given me.

"Ooo you should put on some dark eye liner with your hair slicked wet like that," Evie said, and pulled out her make-up kit. She helped me with the eyeliner and when she was done I felt like I looked different, pretty almost. My eyes were smoky and I was pleased that I could hide behind them. My hair wouldn't look like much by the end of the day since getting it wet meant it would probably wave, but I wasn't going to stand beneath the hand dryer for half an hour with my comb for a half-straight, half-wavy mound of frizz.

Walking down the hallway again there were people casting me sympathetic glances. One of the girls in my science class, Pam, even stopped in the hallway. "You look great Anya," she said with a smile.

"Thanks," I said smiling back.

As I walked down the hall, I spotted Rayne and Pearl making their way over to me.

"Anya, are you okay?" Rayne asked subtly.

"I'm fine," I replied, my eyes letting her know that everything had been taken care of and she shouldn't worry.

"Well you look great Anya. We knew we had to find you when we heard the rumours flying about what happened in the cafeteria today."

"I totally wish I had been there to throw that coffee right back in Gina's face." Pearl said. Something about Gina always seemed to bring out her violent side, which was comedic being how peaceful Pearl was.

"You and me both!" Leah said.

Pearl smiled at her. Rayne smiled too and then spoke to them.

"Thanks Leah and Evie for helping Anya out when we weren't there." She had a saddened expression on her face I knew was the result of feeling guilty. Leah and Evie both looked surprised that Rayne knew their names, especially since she was considered to be a pretty, and popular senior. My human friends suddenly glowed from the small amount of recognition and I was happy for them.

"Of course we would help out our coffee covered girl." Evie said with enthusiasm.

I wrinkled my nose playfully at her.

"Oh it wasn't that bad anyway. You couldn't have known she would plan to attack me Rayne," I said. Then I sent a comforting light cloud of emotion to her before she could even apologize, which wiped away any bad feelings she had.

Rayne and Pearl both hugged me and I laughed. "We're so lucky to have a sister like you."

Pearl said, but then bit her lip when she realized she shouldn't have said that in front of Evie and Leah.

"Well we're like sisters," she said explaining her words.

"Absolutely," Leah said, "we feel the same way about Anya."

Rayne and Pearl looked relieved, but I didn't think they had much to worry about. For a moment we were all in a cloud of happiness, and then I felt eyes on the back of my neck. Someone was staring at me and pelting rays of hatred towards the back of my head. I had quite a hunch about whom.

When I turned I could see Gina leaning against some lockers halfway down the hall. Her friends were with her and Merrick was at her side. Her eyes were fixed on me in a deathly glare and so were Merrick's eyes, only his had something wistful about them. I was thankful for the makeup I had put on, it felt like it was a mask I could hide behind.

When Merrick looked at me with such intensity like that, it left shivers along my spine and I felt like I could have melted. I turned away from them brushing back the waves in my face, but I knew I shouldn't fuss because they immediately fell forward again into my eyes. There was no point in trying to mend things with Gina this early. I could tell there was no way she would agree to a peace.

Chapter 10

THE WEEKEND WAS MY favourite part of the week and it was almost here again. I had managed to live down the rest of the week at school without anyone mentioning "the Gina incident". In fact, I had several sympathetic words from classmates and they mentioned that each year there was an anti-bullying rally at the school they felt I should lead. By Wednesday, people were far too busy thinking about mid-terms.

It felt like it took forever for school let out, but then I could spend time doing what I wanted in hiding, away from everyone. I had a paper to work on, but I had completed most of the research during the early week. I had delved into it on Tuesday to distract myself from the sick and weird love triangle that I had found myself in the midst.

My parents had mentioned to me that our new neighbour was looking for someone to help her with a few things in her bookstore downtown and that I should speak to her about having a little job on the side. Of course I knew that it wouldn't be an actual part-time job, probably just a few things needed to be tidied or sorted, or maybe even re-priced, but if it meant being paid, then I was definitely interested. I was trying to save up money for an e-reader and if my parents didn't decide to buy me one for my birthday any little bit would help.

 So tonight I pulled on my boots, scarf and jacket and slipped my fingers into the red mittens that my mother had bought me. I was trying to add a slight bit of colour to my usually dark attire. It was a short trek across the yards. The muddy earth beneath my feet was similar to a mix of clay causing the brown to seem lifeless and grey. I kicked up a few pebbles closing my eyes and breathing in the moisture of the cool autumn day. It would rain later, I could feel it, and knew that soon it would be ice and snow meeting the ground instead.

 The white porch had paint peeling from its surface and bits of wood grain peeked out from beneath its curling and bubbling twists. As she opened the glass door I observed my neighbour closely. Mrs. Keller had long gray curly hair and dark brown eyes. Her nose was small and pert and her high cheekbones quite striking and symbolic of her beauty.

 "Hello there Anya," she said pushing her hair back off her forehead. "It is nice to finally meet you my dear, though I suppose we've seen one another in the yard and said our hellos."

 Walking into her home, I could smell something baking in the oven, something that smelled delicious and sweet. I took a moment to observe my surroundings as I removed each boot. The walls were a mossy green, and there were periwinkle blue coloured pillows on her neutral couch and love seat. The curtains looked like they were crocheted in a shade of beige very similar to her sofa and there were lacquered wooden furniture pieces in white and baby blue. What I liked most about her home was that it still felt fresh despite its vintage decor.

  She invited me in and offered me a seat in the kitchen, as I walked past the living room a trunk caught my eye. Its entire surface was encrusted with seashells in a beautiful swirl of pattern. Above it a chandelier had oyster shells enchantingly dangling from its surface. I wished that I could run my fingers over the textured surface of each object to feel the residue of the ocean, but it would seem odd.

  "Want a chocolate chip cookie?" She asked removing the plastic wrap from the top of a green ceramic plate.

  "Yes please," I said, my stomach grumbling, even though I had eaten an hour prior.

  "Well aren't you a cutie. Saying please and all," She said to me and I smiled from her infectious warmth.

  "Thank you. I'm too skinny," I admitted before I thought about my confession. The chocolate was warm and melted on my tongue and for a moment I tasted a hint of cinnamon before it was gone.

  "Well, that will change soon enough, take two," she said with a wink. Her earrings glinted from the light shining in through the window and I noticed that they were silver shaped fish with beaded scales.

  "I think your earrings are lovely," I said.

  Her long nimble fingers ran over them causing a tingle of music to float into the room. Her grey cat hopped down from the counter and stretched out eyeing me as though I was a threat. It must have sensed my affinity for water, though it wasn't like I could manipulate it from thin air.

She laughed, "Oh, well, I've had these for ages. And don't mind Alvin there, he just gets finicky when all my attention is not devoted to him. So I hear you like to read, Anya?"

"I love to read." I admitted.

"Well, I own a bookstore in Upper Tantallon, just a small little shop I run a few days during the week, and my son takes care of the rest of the time."

"Oh lovely." I said not really knowing what would be an appropriate response.

"Yes, it is a lovely little place. Anyway I'm looking for someone to help me organize the and sort through the piles of stock my son keeps finding for us when its not needed. I can't walk down an aisle without knocking over twenty books."

"That would be kind of a pain." I said.

"You're telling me little lady." She replied with a twinkle in her eye.

"Anyway Anya, your dad tells me you're a good helper, so I'm wondering if for the next couple of Sundays, you wouldn't mind spending a few hours with me to sort through it all."

"I'd love to," I replied. My fingers started to tingle at the thought of going through all of those books and finding gems hidden in the piles. Immediately, I started to wonder about first editions and old romance paperbacks with outdated dialogue.

"Great," she said with a smile.

ON SUNDAY I BROUGHT my camera with me. There was nothing I loved more than taking photographs of old books, especially hard covers. I had asked Mrs. Keller, the day before, if it would be alright and she had agreed immediately, saying that perhaps I could help her put some of the photographs on the website she had started for the store.

I admired Mrs. Keller, she was flexible and ever changing and when she looked at me it was as though she saw the same quality in me. We had managed to get through half of the boxes in the first two hours and had neatly placed them in piles near their appropriate section in the store, then we decided to take a tea break. Mrs. Keller had an ample supply of tea, I settled on blueberry while she filled the kettle.

In addition to paying me ten dollars an hour, Mrs. Keller had graciously offered for me to pick five books that I wanted, free of charge. I didn't know why she was being quite so nice to me, but I appreciated it, and worked quickly and harder for her as a result. She pulled out a few mugs and I dropped our teabags into them.

"So your mother tells me you have a boyfriend, Anya." I looked at her, surprised my mother had said anything about Merrick to anyone.

"Not exactly," I replied. I hadn't ever called Merrick my boyfriend, nor had I really considered the notion.

"Not exactly?" She asked amused, crow's feet spreading out on her face with her smile. "I suppose things rarely are what they appear to be." She continued on, "Especially with the other sex. Males are tricky, but when you find a good one, you'll know."

"Let's hope so." I said.

"Ahh, well you have to kiss a few frogs before you meet your prince." She chuckled. "That much I tell you is true."

We sat while the tea steeped, taking a break from shifting the books around and bending to lift piles and piles of them.

"So you like romance and adventure?" Mrs.

Keller asked me, noticing the titles of the three books I had gathered and placed as my potential freebies.

"Yes, I really do." I said with a smile.

"Oh well then, what would be your ideal adventure Anya?"

"My ideal adventure?" I had considered it many times before, probably too many times. I wanted to swim the waters of the world, to explore oceans, and rivers, and lakes, and learn more about the Mer communities there.

"If you could leave tomorrow, with a pile of money, and do anything you want, what would it be?"

I couldn't say swim to each and every Atlantean city, so I settled for what would seem most appropriate to say. "I would sail the world. Explore the rivers and oceans; maybe study the wildlife."

She smiled at me. "Makes sense that you're a photographer then." She was right I did like taking photos, though I hardly considered myself an actual artist.

"I have something you would like," she said rubbing her index finger along her mouth. "I don't show it to many people, because it's been waiting for the right person to come in here for it, and I'm starting to think that it just might be you, Anya. I saw the way you admired my chandelier and trunk. You're drawn to the ocean like I am." She disappeared into a small closet next to the cash and returned with something wrapped in string and thick parchment paper.

Setting it on the table a pile of dust flew out from the folds in the paper and I realized that it really had been there for quite some time. I reached forward to help her undo the twine and when she gingerly pulled back the paper to reveal the cover, I nearly gasped aloud in shock. The cover of the book was a seal pelt with an inner square on the front in mother of pearl. Black inky swirls of Mecrutian writing carved into the front of it, read Enchantments of Time and Disposition and around the square were individual pearls bordering like a frame.

"I'm not sure what the language is, Anya, but it looks to me like it might be something in between Cyrillic and Sanskrit. Perhaps those parents of yours might be able to help you with deciphering some of it."

"It's absolutely breathtaking," I managed to say.

"Oh you haven't even opened the cover yet," she said amused, "you should see the paintings inside." Flipping open the cover, there was a word written in Mercrutian, *llyruio,* or as we would say modernly, a *grimoire.* There were beautiful drawings of Mers and sea life- intricate paintings of fish and dolphins. I ran my fingers over the melding colours impressed with how well preserved the book was.

"When did you find this?" I asked wondering if she had any indication of what a treasure she had found.

"A very long time ago my dear," she said and then immediately began re-wrapping it up. "You mustn't tell anyone, but your parents about it Anya, it's a treasure to be guarded. You understand?" She asked firmly.

"I do," I replied, suddenly wondering just how much she knew about Mers and Atlanteans. This book had given her a glimpse into our world and I couldn't gather whether or not she believed we existed.

"Thank you," I whispered, taking the book from her hands. "I promise to protect it dutifully."

"You're a good girl Anya. I know you will."

How Mrs. Keller had known to give me such a gem, I didn't know, but I was incredibly thankful for her brilliance.

Chapter 11

My dentist appointment was right after school and I had anticipated it with excitement and apprehension. My mother had even taken the afternoon off of work just so that she could drive me there. It was a weird present for my birthday, but having straight teeth was one of the best things I could have hoped for; to be free of my braces would be such a reward.

Tomorrow Evelyn and Leah would come over. After the weekend of fun that I had with the Prices two weeks earlier, I was really looking forward to another night with my friends. I had asked them if they wanted to go into Halifax for shopping, which seemed like the thing that girls our age did, but they said they preferred to chill at my house. We would have a movie marathon with goodies, and I was eager to try out the black nail polish Pearl had given me, which I hadn't opened yet. We had already bought snacks and my mother had surprised me with seaweed chips. I knew it probably wasn't the kind of thing that the other girls would like, but I loved them and could eat a whole bag in one sitting.

My tongue glided over my teeth surprised by the smoothness there. They were still a little bit sensitive from the chalky feeling of having the brackets removed. My mouth was so dry that I was grateful my mother had brought a large jug of water with her, and I drank eagerly from it before I flipped down the mirror in the car and looked at my teeth again. The dental assistant had handed me a hand mirror that I had gazed into briefly, but now I could really examine them. My teeth were perfectly straight. Between my smile and my eyebrows, and my hair growing longer, it was a weird face staring back at me.

"What do you think Anya?" My mother asked.

"I think it's great. I can't wait to eat some Junior Caramels…Oh, and to chew gum again. Oh gum, how I love thee."

She laughed. "We'll pick some up on the way home."

I chewed on the caramels slowly, my jaw was immediately sore from the unexpected motion. Yet, even though my gums were a little tender, I felt great. A little while later, I sat on my bed with a book in my lap and my box of caramels at my side in pure heaven.

My mom walked into the room with the phone and handed it to me.

"Who is…"

She mouthed a name I didn't quite catch, and then the voice on the other line was already speaking.

"Hello Anya." It was a male's voice, but seemingly unrecognizable.

"Hi," I said trying to wrack my brain in recognition, it wasn't Merrick. It wasn't Seth.

"It's Zale." He said as if reading my mind.
"Zale! Hi! How are you?"
"I'm well." He spoke softly. "I would like to see you."
"Me?" I asked surprised by his formal tone.
"Yes, may I come over?"
"Of course," I said not seeing a reason why he shouldn't, everything for the party had already been prepared and the only thing I had planned that night was to maybe watch an episode of that H2O show that I liked so much.
"Perfect," he said, and then hung up. I felt jarred by the suddenness of his actions. Not even a minute later the doorbell rang. Clumsily I made my way down the stairs and to the door. When I opened it, there was Zale's blonde spiky haired head. *How on earth did he get here so fast I wondered?* Only there was not amusement at my surprise on his face. His blue eyes were pale and his face looked tired.
"Come in," I said. "Did you teleport here?" I asked jokingly.
"Something like that." He answered as he examined his surroundings. "Your house is nice." My parents had quickly decorated the walls with their worldly wares, and tapestries from their travels before I was born. My mother had such an affinity for ornate things that I was surprised he hadn't supplemented the word 'gaudy' for nice.
"Thanks. Thirsty?"
"No," he said as he removed his shoes and then unzipped his bomber jacket. For a moment I noticed that he looked a little older.
"Have you begun transcending?" I blurted out unable to contain myself.
He looked at me; his expression pained as though he knew his answer would hurt me.

"Yes." He replied and winced when my face fell. "Anya it will happen for you, I promise you that," his hand reached out to grab mine and he held it tenderly.

"I have something for you," he said and unzipped his jacket pulling out a thin book like object wrapped in purple shimmering decorative paper. "A birthday present. Happy Birthday Anya."

I smiled, touched from the bottom of my heart. He was so very sweet. It pained me to see him so distraught. We moved towards the front room and sat down on the couch there. The room was hardly ever used, but it was handy and had plenty of seating. I took the present from him and unwrapped it slowly, trying to preserve the paper so that I could reuse it later for something else. When I finished unwrapping it I realized it was a leather cover for a book and opening it up I was shocked when I saw that tucked into the cover was an e-reader.

Zale smiled slowly. "I thought you might like it."

"Zale, you bought this for me?" My heart fluttered, the gesture was unbelievable and overwhelming. The emotions from him were warm and comforting, his love and care for me in that moment were so clear, but unexpected.

"Well Merrick helped, a lot." He admitted and laughed.

"He did?" I asked surprised.

"Yeah, like ninety percent. We both wanted you to have a really good birthday this year."

"How did you know this was what I wanted?" I asked.

He simply tapped the side of his head. "It's all in here," he said.

I looked at him for a moment wondering

exactly what that meant, and then I realized that I could ask him.

"I think maybe you should tell me about that. C'mon," I said coyly and grabbed his hand leading him to the kitchen. "I'll make us some hot chocolate and we can have a good chat."

He sat at the kitchen island and interlaced his fingers, resting them on the wooden place mats my mother had purchased. Instead of using water I pulled out some milk, it would make the drink much richer. I grabbed the chocolate powder and marshmallows, as well as some extra baking chocolate I could melt into the mixture.

"You're going to spoil me with that delicious drink." Zale said breaking the comfortable silence between us. He sounded like Merrick.

I looked over at him as I turned on the burner and placed the pot on the stove. He was looking at me the same way Merrick did whenever we were alone. There was curiosity beneath the surface of something else that I couldn't decipher. Emotionally he was bare, and so I could read nothing from him. Then, his eyes began to change in the light and they faded and cooled into something closer to grey. In that moment, seeing him there with his eyes like that and his face calmly serene, I wanted to move closer to him and touch him somewhere, anywhere that his skin was bare. I yearned to place my hand against his cheek. I felt such a deep kinship with him that I could not explain. It wasn't desire or something purely platonic, instead it was as though we were connected, as though we should be touching.

I thought of Merrick and wondered what this meant. If I felt this way for his brother was it wrong? Even though I had felt similar things for Merrick, only they were far more passionate; I couldn't help but wonder where this emotion stemmed from when it was clearly different than my bond with the Price females.

"What would you like for me to tell you, Anya?" He asked almost flirtatiously.

"Well what would you like to tell me, Zale?" I asked matching his tone. He was so easy to be near that I felt comforted by his presence. He chuckled and I felt him relax even more.

"Well for starters there are always going to be some things that I'll know which will make you wonder how I knew them."

"You have the gift of telepathy?" I asked, "And you can somehow move quickly from one place to another...teleportation."

"Teleportation, yes, but only through water. And well, to your telepathy question, no." He answered, watching me place the mug on the place mat in front of him and turn the handle towards him. "Thank you, Anya." He added.

"You're welcome." I answered. "So then... you *cannot* read my thoughts?" I said wanting to confirm that I was in the clear.

"No," he said with a smile, blowing lightly on the drink and pushing a large marshmallow down with his finger. "Sometimes I wish I could though," He said and then winked at me.

"You wouldn't want to be up there in that jumbled mess of my mind," I said grabbing my own cup and sitting next to him. "You said teleportation through water. How is that?"

"It's hard to explain. It's like the water splits me apart molecularly and I can jump from source to source. I know that doesn't make much sense, but that's the best explanation I have."

"No," I began, "that I can understand, even if

it does not make sense in human rules of the universe- I understand how that could fit into the Mer world. We're an enchanted society, so, water travel makes sense."He took another sip and licked the chocolate from his lips before he answered.

"Good. So you like your gift?" He asked looking at it on the counter top between us. Then I realized I hadn't even thanked him!

"Yes I love it! Thank you so much." I said and hugged him soundly. "I'm sorry, I was so curious about your powers, I forgot my manners."

He shook his head in disbelief, but there was still a smile plastered on his face. "You are always polite Anya, no need to apologize." I looked at him with a smile but I still felt a little nervous about his powers. I wondered what else he could do and how he did it.

"So then what is it, what allows you to know things sometimes?" I asked wondering if I was starting to annoy him with my determined questioning.

"I just, see things..." He said with a shrug.

"Like visions?" I chose the word carefully.

"Yes." He said and gave me a look that made me want to fill in the blank.

"Of the future?" I guessed, my voice unsure as I spoke.

"Yes."

"Hmmm... no wonder you looked so distressed the other day," I said and placed my hand over his in comfort. His hand turned up to mine and he squeezed it gently.

"I can see why my brother is so in love with you," he said softly under his breath.

I jerked my hand back surprised by his words. "What did you say Zale?"

He looked up at me and the corner of his mouth pulled up slightly. "You heard me."

"*You* said Merrick *loves* me." I spoke in an accusatory tone. I wanted to point at him for emphasis, but held back.

His look remained remarkably calm. "Yes."

"I don't think you know what you're talking about Zale." As far as I knew, none of the Prices knew why Merrick had picked me, and it seemed peculiar considering they were all quite close. "Your brother didn't pick me to be his betrothed because he loves me."

"No, he didn't. He picked you because I asked him to."

"What do you mean you asked him to?"

"It's a long story Anya and I don't have time to tell it all, but whatever he says to you, whatever even I might say to you, now or later. You two were meant. He loves you, and will love you always, more than I ever could."

"I don't believe you Zale." I felt hurt and confused by what he was saying. What did he mean 'no matter what he said to me' and 'more than he ever could'?

"He *does* love you Anya, though right now he may not show it," Zale took my hand this time and held it.

"No," I said shaking my head in disbelief. "He wants to be with Gina."

"For now," he acquiesced, "maybe I might love you more. Well right now in this moment, I think."

I swallowed hard, staring into his eyes speechless. *Why would he say that?* We hardly knew one another, and hadn't he just told me to disregard what he might say?

"You love me?" I whispered so low that I wondered if he understood.

"Oh hello, Zale," my mother said walking into the kitchen and pulling a carton of juice from the fridge.

"Hello Mrs. Patel, you're looking beautiful today." Zale was smiling with the same charm I had seen Merrick turn on half a dozen times since first meeting him.

"Oh, why thank you Zale, you're such a sweetheart." She glanced at our hands, mine still being held by his. "Would you like to stay for supper?"

"No thank you, but I really appreciate the offer. I must be going now actually." Zale got up from his seat.

"Okay," my mom replied. "Well hope that you have a good evening, Zale, come over any time."

"I'll see you out." I said, finally regaining my voice, I followed him to the door. "Do you really have to go?" I asked trying to think of a way to get him to stay. We had just begun scratching the surface with our conversation and I felt like there was so much more to be said, so much more that he wanted to tell me.

"I can't," he said tying his laces, "but believe me, I want to. I have to go away for a little while Anya, but I promise I'll come back."

"What do you mean you're going away?" I asked suddenly feeling a rush of emotion that had me bereft and cold.

"Hey there, Zale," my father said walking by the entryway on his way to the kitchen. "I hear congratulations are in order. You received that prestigious nine month internship with the Sealatian Order in the main Atlantian city."

My father reached out and shook Zale's hand. I

blew out a breath, exasperated that everyone kept interrupting my conversation with him, each time I felt like he was telling me something incredibly important.

"Thanks Mr. Patel," he replied and pushed back his hair off his face. "I'm looking forward to my time in the blue. It's a little dry here for me." He said and winked.

"Don't I know what you mean," my father said laughing and patted him on the back. They were joking, at a time like this? Zale had just confessed that not only Merrick loved me, or would love m,e or something along those lines but more importantly he loved me too, and that he could teleport, and see into the future, and apparently was leaving for the ocean, and *most importantly* that he loved me! My head was beginning to hurt, I wanted to have this all sorted out. I shot my dad a look and he glanced back and forth between us.

"Well take care Tiger Shark," he said to Zale, then turned to me. "I'm going to go see if your mother needs help with supper,Anya."

"Okay Dad," I said and watched him until he was out of sight. I had grabbed Zale's sleeve half-expecting him to disappear, while I waited to make sure my dad was out of earshot.

"You can't drop all of those things on me, and tell me you love me, and then just leave like you'll be stopping by tomorrow when you're leaving for nine months Zale, that's just not fair." I crossed my arms clearly demanding some answers.

He smiled sweetly, but I didn't budge and grabbed his sleeve again when he moved to the door.

"Don't leave Zale," I said pulling him into a hug.

He hugged me back and rocked me a little in comfort. "I'm running out of time Anya. Look I can tell you this much. I might love you more than Merrick at this particular moment, but he's going to love you a whole lot more in the time to come. The teleporting and future seeing are things you're just going to have to accept. The future is tricky business. I can only see so far ahead and even then it's only once someone close is faced with a choice. And then, even if I do see things it doesn't always mean they're right." He stroked my cheek in comfort and for that moment it felt as though everything thing he said was true, everything *would* be as he said. Then I thought about it all.

"You said sometimes things you see aren't right. So then maybe Merrick won't love me like you say."

"No," he said and shook his head as though I were way off base. "That's not possible. That- I am completely right about."

I looked into his eyes and he seemed so sure of himself, so confident that he was speaking the truth about Merrick and me.

"What if you're wrong?" For a moment I saw a flicker of doubt in his eyes and then he frowned.

"I wish I was wrong." He whispered. "Remember what you told me that night at my house? You said you would help me, Anya."

"I will," I said eagerly. "I promise, but you need to tell me how."

"When the time is right you'll know. The voice inside you will guide you to me."

"What? What does that mean Zale?" Then the timer on his watch started beeping and he looked at me saddened.

"I'm out of time, Anya. I'll be back." He cupped my face and kissed me softly on the lips. My heart pounded only I couldn't tell if was out of guilt or emotional connection. *What was with the Price boys and kissing me?!*

"Zale!?" I cried pulling back with wide eyes.

He smirked. "I couldn't help it, you're so cute." He opened the door and walked out. The moment his shoe touched a pool of water on the porch, he was gone and once again I was feeling confused.

He dissolved into the water? Wait, he thought I was cute?

Chapter 12

I had a sinking feeling, the type of dreaded feeling you get when something goes wrong. A jolt of pain shot through my leg causing me to jerk up. I opened my eyes slowly. I was in my room lying on my bed and glanced at the clock by the nightstand. It was seven o'clock in the evening. I sat up feeling hazy. *Had I been dreaming?* I could have sworn that Zale had come over.

Even though the air in the room was cold I shook back the covers and got out of bed, stretching out into my dark room. I slid my feet into my slippers and prepared to make my way downstairs. *Where was the e-reader that Zale and Merrick had bought me?* I rubbed my neck and walked zombie-like down the hallway.

"There's my girl!" My father said as I walked into the kitchen.

"How long was I out for?" I asked him, looking

around the room for any signs that Zale had actually visited.

"Not long," he replied, maybe half an hour. "Since we're celebrating your birthday tomorrow with pizza while your friends are over, your mother thought tonight we could just have a nice cooked meal. We made some fish and fixings in the oven."

"Yeah, that sounds great, Dad." I said and yawned while I walked over to the sink and glanced into it, there was no sign of the pot or the cups that I had used to make the hot chocolate. I even checked the dish tray and none of them were there.

"What are you looking for Anya?"

"Was Zale here?" I asked.

"The youngest Price boy?"

"Yeah..." I said and rubbed my face with my hand.

"No, but Caspian stopped in on his way to Atlantis. He left that for you." My eyes followed my father's hand to the counter there was a large gold gift bag there with matching decorative tissue spilling out of the top.

"For me?" I walked over to it and pulled on the tissue gingerly. There was a beautiful black cashmere sweater with a ribbon around it and a tag stating that it was from Ondine and Caspian. Beneath that there was a box with a sparkly red beaded bracelet and a beautiful purple scarf. There was also some make up, some nail polish and some other goodies which were marked as being from Coral, Pearl, and Rayne. Then, beneath that, was a leather book cover, just like the one in my dream. My hand trembled when I reached for it and my mother, who had joined us in the kitchen, gasped at how beautiful it was.

"My Anya, that's gorgeous."

"Very nice indeed," my father said in agreement.

Written across the tag were the names Zale and Merrick, but if my dream had been right then I knew that Merrick had spent a lot of his money on me. Maybe it wasn't an e-reader, maybe it was just a book. I unwrapped the leather tie, thinking a book would suit me just fine, but the moment I began I knew, it was the one thing I had really wanted. As I looked at the screen I thought I might collapse to the floor, but the dramatic display would only have my parents worried.

How could I have dreamed this very thing before it had happened? And exactly what else about my dream had been true. My mind was starting to dissect everything that had happened while I'd slept and I raced into the office grabbing a pen and paper to write it all down.

"Anya, what are you doing?" My parents asked simultaneously.

"I'll be right back," I said still holding the e-reader to my heart. I scribbled quickly trying to remember every minute detail, the inflection in his voice each time Zale had spoken, and what he had said about Merrick. When I returned to the kitchen my parents looked at me oddly, they had begun arranging our food on the table.

"Everything okay?" My dad asked stroking my hair.

"Yes," I said, "I'm going to have to write 'Thank You' cards for these wonderful gifts."

"That's a great idea Anya." My mother replied, placing our glasses of water on the table.

Only I didn't know what or how I would start writing to Merrick or Zale and I was beginning to wonder if I should write to them both separately.

I was too tired and too hungry to think straight, so I reasoned that I had a long day and was maybe out of sorts. At least I had written the dream down to reference later. Since I could do nothing at the present moment about Zale, or Merrick, I would eat, rest, and tackle things first thing in the morning.

I FINISHED WRITING MY thank you letters early in the morning, and spent the rest of the it trying to distract myself from thoughts of Merrick and Zale. My parents had given me a few presents the night before, an outfit for school, which looked like my usual dark blue jeans and black sweater and a gift card to buy more books. So, I searched online to see if there were any titles that I wanted to purchase.

It was no use though after a few minutes I grew restless and couldn't sit still, because all I could see were the visions of Merrick and Zale intermittently. Anytime I closed my eyes, they were there haunting me. So then I spent hours looking over the *grimoire* that Mrs. Keller had unknowingly given me, flipping through the pages in the hopes that I could find some Mer information on time travel, and water teleportation.

What was written about it was limited, and the whole thing was in an older dialect of Mer that was more difficult to transcribe. What I had managed to decipher was something close to a fog creating potion that allowed you to enter the mist and arrive somewhere else. It was odd to think that my dream of Zale had preceded my knowledge of that kind of Mer magic. I guessed that perhaps I had tapped into some sort of shared "Mer essence" to learn about it, which made sense for our species and its emotional capabilities.

There were many diagrams of Mers and as I flipped through the pages I fell upon one that looked so similar to Merrick, I stopped. Its uncanny resemblance had even managed to capture the same slightly rebellious inflection in his eyes. The portrait was a little older in appearance, but the top of the page had an inscription relating to a hero. Regrettably there was little of the passage I could decipher. For nearly half an hour I had been captivated with the image, though, and admired the details.

    Near the end of the book there was another one that stood out to me. It was something about going back in time to change the path of a loved one. That one had many warnings written above it, and so seemed like it was not something to be conjured lightly. Even the pages looked foreboding. On one side was watercolour with a pale blue sky, darkening to a greyish black as it met the horizon. It was a seascape with a lighthouse; the light from the structure captured by a speckled coating of shimmering dust. I gathered that it was some kind of sparkly paint used with a thin brush. On the opposite side was the transcription flanked by a diagram of a Mer with a navy blue cape, hooded, so that there was no way to distinguish any features of the face. Behind the figure, wisps of the grey depths seemed to reach out,and curl about it in a thick cloud. As I looked at the page, it was almost as if I could see the smoke move and I jumped when I heard the doorbell, I suspected it was my friends and went to the door to meet them, but it was too early.

    Instead a postman had arrived with a letter for my father and mother. A large navy envelope with gold seals, clearly something from the Mer Institute of Science, I took it gingerly wondering what the contents would hold. They quietly looked at each other when I handed it to them, but no words were exchanged. I had an uneasy feeling about the envelope, but couldn't find the right words to ask what it meant.

EVELYN AND LEAH ARRIVED around three o'clock and I was pretty excited that they had both shown up early. I was grateful that they had finally come over because I needed the distraction from my recent dream and my growing feelings for Merrick. The book had been enchanting and had broken up my confusion about the dream with Zale, but even then the one image on the hero page was so hauntingly similar to my teal eyed Mer that it had only calmed my mind for so long.

I still couldn't believe he had bought me an e-reader and not just any one either; it was the top of the line for that particular model. It made me euphoric just thinking about it, but then I had a thought that perhaps he hadn't bought it- maybe his parents had. I scowled to myself. I was wrong, or right, I didn't know and the only way to find out for certain was to speak with him, but that I knew wouldn't happen for some time. Mostly, I was just grateful. The next week at school would be exam week, followed by our Christmas break. So the opportunity to see him would be in the future.

Thankfully, with Evie and Leah around, I could shift my thoughts to something else. Or so I had thought, until they positioned themselves on my bed, and pulled out a yearbook from the previous year at the high school.

"Where did you get that?" I asked knowing that both of them had started high school that very year, like me.

Evie looked over at Leah with a dubious smile. "Leah's older brother Garrett went to Sir John A last year, before graduating and he somehow ended up with two yearbooks by mistake. So this one here pilfered it, and scribbled notes next to all the cute boys."

I laughed, and then swallowed thinking about Merrick's picture. *What would he have looked like then?* Probably not too much different than he did now, he looked like he had begun his transformation much younger.

Leah squealed when she opened the cover to a page bookmarked with a neon pink sticky note. "Oh my goodness! That Merrick Price is one delish dish."

My cheeks heated in a blush. "You think so?" I asked trying not to give any hints at my feelings for him.

Evie smiled, "Yeah, but Murdock and Kai are more my type. Mmm mmm who doesn't like a bad boy?"

Leah snorted. "Um me!" She raised her hand. "I think Hurley's my favourite, with his copper curls and baby blues. I love that dimple in his chin!"

"What about you, Anya? Which guy knocks your socks off?"

"Umm none of them," I replied with a shrug.

"See! I told you she didn't like Merrick!" Leah said to Evie, with a pat on her arm.

"I could have sworn she did," Evie said looking at me.

I laughed nervously.

"You do!" Leah exclaimed, pointing at me.

"I...I..."

"It's okay," Evie said, "we kind of figured you did since we always see you with Rayne and Pearl. One of these days, you gotta tell us how you managed to swing an in with them."

"Our parents are friends," I said using the same excuse that Merrick had given Gina.

"Lucky!" Evie said flipping the page of the year

book.

"He's got to like you back at least a little bit," Leah started saying with a fishy look on her face, "otherwise G-dog wouldn't have gone on the war path against you."

"It's complicated," I admitted. "We're friends."

"Friends who sometimes kiss?" Evie asked looking up at me teasingly.

"What?" I asked completely stunned. They both smiled as though they had caught me red handed.

Excitedly she sat up on my bed. "So— the other day we were sitting in on the grade ten advanced Math class at the back of the room, trying to decide if we were brainy enough to enrol and of course with our luck. Thank the heavens! We were seated just behind the table where Merrick, Kai, Hurley, and Murdock sat."

My jaw dropped open. "Merrick told them!"

"Not in so many words," Leah said. "It's true!? He kissed you?"

"Oh Mother of Pearl! Why would he tell them?" I said loudly and while Evie and Leah exchanged excited looks I paced back and forth.

"Oh my gosh! He kissed you!!" Leah exclaimed.

"Here's what happened," Evie started. "Merrick strolled into class, later than the other guys, and joined the rest of the hotties at the table."

"Then," Leah said taking over, "Murdock said some wisecrack about Merrick making out with you while Gina was on a rampage looking for him."

"Then, Merrick said that he was not making out with you at that moment, so she needed to chill, because lately her freak outs were getting worse and the guys were not doing anything to help the situation," Evie said take over again. "But, Kai, because he's brilliant and I love him, so much, realized what Merrick said and asked, 'What do you mean at that moment?'"

"To which, like a jackass Murdock said 'ewww sick'" Leah said shaking her head in disapproval. "And she wonders why I don't like the bad boys," she said to me giving Evie a look. Evie replied with a comical facial expression and a jutting tongue.

"Then, Merrick, in defending your honour told Murdock to shut up and smacked him across the back of his head, saying that kissing you was actually nicer than being choked by Gina's new tongue piercing!" Evie finished excitedly. "Oh and Kai, because he's so cute said, 'At least Merrick is kissing someone!' Which was definitely a jab directed towards Murdock."

Part of me was happy that Merrick hadn't told them outright and had defended me when Murdock made fun, but another part of me was mortified that they knew. And, a little worried that Gina would find out, and make another move to try and slaughter me socially.

"Oh." I said growing quiet.

"Well don't hold out on us Anya!! What was it like? Tell us!" I didn't think that Leah's voice could rise to a higher pitch, but apparently it could.

"Come on! Details!" Evie added, "did he French kiss you?"

"No!" I said feeling embarrassed while I covered my face, but still had giggles rapidly pouring out of me.

"Anya, please let us live through you!" Leah was so excited.

"Well," I began, peeking through my fingers. "It was sweet. It was... unexpected. We were just sort of chilling, and I was talking a mile a minute, which I think annoyed him a little. So he just leaned in and kissed me, three times."

"Were his lips soft or were they like jagged plastic?" Leah asked.

I laughed. "Plastic huh? No. They were soft."

"Oooooo" Evie said tossing herself back on my pillows. "Dreamy!"

Leah completed the same motion, and finally, I wedge myself between them so that all of us were staring at my ceiling.

"Do you think I'll ever get to kiss Kai? I'd French kiss him any day." Evie asked.

"Maybe...you never know," I said. "Kissing complicates things though. Sometimes I wish Merrick hadn't kissed me."

"Oh does it now?" Leah asked. "So he just did it huh? Was he suave, or powerful, or charming."

"He was probably charming." Evie answered for me, "he usually is."

"He was... tender" I thought back to that moment. *Was there any particular way that he had acted? Not really.* "He smiled at me, he had already moved closer to me because we were talking and then he cupped my cheek with his hand and kissed me."

"What's so complicated about that?" Leah asked.

"Everything." I said not caring to elaborate.

"Clearly, he likes you," Evie added.

"Yeah... maybe. You guys want to get some snacks?" I asked, hoping we could get away from the subject of boys.

"I brought Earl Grey flavoured cupcakes with me, covered in butter cream frosting, courtesy of my, Ma." Leah said grabbing the open page of the yearbook with Hurley on it and holding it close to her chest.

"That sounds perfect!" I said and hopped up from the bed, my mouth could already taste the fluffiness in contrast with the sweet frosting and I could almost smell the rich Bergamot oil. Leah and Evie were still laying there staring at the ceiling.

"Are you guys coming?" I asked wondering why they would dawdle.

Evie spoke, "Anya, if you go out with Merrick, will you put in a good word for us with his hot friends?" They both sat up and looked at me hopefully.

"Of course I would." I answered. "But, don't expect that to be happening anytime soon, cause I sure as heck don't think it will."

Evie sighed and looked at Leah. "Well I guess that's better than nothing. Onto the cupcakes!"

Chapter 13

THE SNOWFLAKES OUTSIDE WERE large crystalline spheres floating down steadily. When the wind picked up they swirled in a little dance before meeting the ground and melting. When the weather cooled, there would be piles of snow on the ground. The week before, there had been mounds and mounds of it everywhere and then a wet snow-rain mix had moved in with mild weather and taken most of the white away, leaving things looking a little dreary.

Yet, my surroundings were warm and cheerful. Mrs. Keller had thoroughly decorated her home for the holidays and had lit some pine scented candles, which wafted in the air. Exams were thankfully over, and now it was time for relaxing. I had made all of my presents, and wrapped them, including the ones for the Prices. For all of my girlfriends, Mrs. Keller, Mrs. Price and my mother I had made shell jewellery sets. For the males, I had knitted scarves and mittens to keep them warm during the winter chill. Now I was preparing for a baking-fest, after which I could wrap the cookies I made and give those as gifts too.

"So Anya, have your holidays been pleasant so far?" Mrs. Keller asked.

"Yeah, they've been really great." I said lining the cookie sheet with parchment so I could place an assortment of gingerbread shapes on them.

"So how is that boyfriend of yours?" She asked with a twinkle in her eye. "Any less complicated?"

I chuckled. "Not really."

"You know, when I was your age, I was a lot more concerned with boys. It's refreshing to see a girl like you out and doing your own thing. I have a granddaughter who is a little older than you, but at your age. Boy! We couldn't keep track of them!"

"I don't think I'll ever have that problem," I said smiling.

"Oh just you wait, Anya," she began, "you're going to blossom into an even bigger beauty- before you know it, and the guys will be chasing you."

I shook my head smiling. Mrs. Keller always had a way about her that was earnest and warm, but it was always enjoyable when her comedic side came out. She provided me with proverbs and verses on important things in life. I sensed one about to float to the surface.

"One thing that you have to keep in mind though is this," she paused for effect. "Do you want a man to stand in front of you, behind you, or beside you? If you can figure that out, it doesn't matter what else happens, because the right guy will find you. I found my Harold that way, or rather he stumbled across me."

"Well I'm kind of stuck with mine," I said not realizing what I was saying.

"Oh sweetheart, you're never stuck with any

man. Tell me, how does he make you feel? What does he do to treat you right?"

"Well," I began not knowing where to start. "He makes me laugh when we talk. He's usually pretty playful, and mischievous."

"Oh well that can be attractive in a boyfriend, what else?"

"He's usually nice to me, though his teasing does get on my nerves. And he's charming. We banter a lot, he flirts with me."

"Is he flirtatious with all the other girls?" Does he look at them the way that he looks at you?"

I realized for the first time, that I hadn't given much thought to comparing the way Merrick was with me, as opposed to the way he was with Gina. What limited witnessing I had to their conversations, had mostly consisted of Gina speaking at Merrick. In fact, thinking about it, it irked me a little. How dare she talk to him like that! And treat him like a possession, when clearly he was more than just a pretty face. In fact a lot of the girls at school treated him that way. They ogled him whenever he walked down the hall and on more than one occasion when Gina wasn't present, I had seen a few girls throw themselves at him. Yet, he never really rose to the bait.

Mrs. Keller interrupted my musing with her next string of questions. "Well what about the important things? Is he a good kisser?"

I fought back the urge to giggle when she nudged me with her elbow and nodded. "Umm yeah, he's good at that, gentle."

"Ohhh gentle you say. Well that's the sign of a gentleman. Only rogues throw you around like you're some sort of rag doll."

I definitely did not like the sounds of that. Thank goodness Merrick was never rough with me.

We set to work and baked two batches of gingerbread, one of sugar cookies, and three of almond cherry coconut chews. By the end of it, after we had placed the cookies out to cool over every available surface, we both swore we would never eat another cookie for weeks.

Chapter 14

My fingers twirled through my now controllable hair. It was still not the silky and shiny quality of a Mer, but the coarse frizz had been reduced thanks to Rayne's enchanted shampoo, which over the past two months had really worked magic.

Evelyn and Leah had invited me to the Winter Carnival. We had finished with our midterms and since the holidays were over, we were counting the weeks until spring. I could not wait until March break was on the horizon, I looked forward to another week of indulgent reading and relaxation; the Christmas season had ended far too quickly.

Valentine's Day would be in another week and a half. Then there would be the dreaded Valentine's Dance, combined with the winter formal we had missed in December. Leah and Evelyn were still trying to convince me to attend, though I doubted I would make an appearance.

We hadn't been at the carnival for long, just

enough to scope out the ice rink and the few interesting things on the sidelines. There was a stand with Beaver Tails and one with coffee, tea, hot apple cider, and hot chocolate. The smells of cinnamon and cocoa in the air were intoxicating. Nearby, a manmade snow bank was the object of much sledding, and people everywhere were laughing and playing with the snow, making snow angels and building snow people.

    I could see him on the ice. Merrick was dressed in a black pea coat with a long, grey, knitted scarf tossed around his neck. The mild winter chill did not seem bothersome to his face or ears, but they were both covered with layers of his thick dark hair. He didn't have the same ruddy tone as some of the other boys. There were half a dozen other guys skating around him, some of them were even Mers and equally cute, but my eyes were directly drawn to him. He was so handsome and graceful as he skated. I couldn't help but feel pride that he was my mate. We hadn't spoken in a while and with school being so busy. We had merely passed one another in the halls a few times and nodded.

    Sitting with Evelyn and Leah, I didn't want to watch him too closely. They had no idea he was my betrothed and it had to stay that way. It was funny to think that they talked about him and his friends as the dreamy boys who were way out of their league. I suppose I sometimes felt similarly, but knew different. The fact that they knew he had kissed me, had built our camaraderie, and it was nice that I could trust them not to spread the secret. It seemed that, so far, none of the other Mers had too, though Gina had not been any friendlier.

    It was then that his eyes shifted slowly to mine, as though they could feel me watching, the teal of them seemed to brighten. I looked down, my heart suddenly hammering as though I'd been caught doing something bad. When I glanced up again his eyes were still on me, and for a moment I thought he was going to skate over until three or four girls, giggling on the ice cut him off and began talking to him. Gina was one of them and immediately her eyes cut to me, to where Merrick's attention was diverted from her. She gave me a nasty look, one that could have struck a feeble child or small animal dead.

"Gina's such a beotch," Evelyn said with a snarl, breaking my thoughts.

"Yeah, just because we have no chance with the hotties, doesn't mean we can't look right Anya?" Leah added, elbowing me.

I had been doubly caught. Crapbag. I smiled at them weakly and then shrugged. I was tempted to look back at Merrick one more time, but stopped myself. That would be reckless and in an instant would have Gina skate her pretty butt over to me and initiate cat fight, part two. At least Merrick could never complain that I was possessive of him.

Instead, I focused on the ice, after lacing up my skates I realized that this would be a challenge. I was really rusty at skating. In fact, I had only skated once or twice before. At first I felt wobbly and uncontrolled on the ice. My greatest fear was wiping out in front of everyone in the middle of the rink.

I took a deep breath and focused, there was water beneath my feet, it was my home element, and it was calming. I knew that if I exercised control, I could channel my Mer senses to remain balanced. It worked and before long, I was enjoying my amateur skating abilities alongside Evelyn and Leah, who were just as cautious and following a similar pace. We smiled at one another while we skated, and I could tell they felt the same free feeling that I did.

It wasn't until our third lap around the rink that I could feel eyes watching us. I glanced around quickly to see Murdock with Gina, not far from Merrick who was talking animatedly with some of the other male Mers. Gina had whispered something to Murdock, her eyes still locked on me and I fought every bone in my body not to stop right then and there and cower on the ice. *What were they planning this time?* Gina had mortified me enough the last time we had a run in that I knew better to avoid her.

Today, I wouldn't let them get the best of me. I tilted my chin higher and pushed my chest out continuing my skating. Evelyn and Leah, in front of me gestured towards the hot chocolate stand outside the rink and before I could protest were skating off in its direction. They had expected me to follow and turned around watching me continue to skate. They looked at me fearfully on the sidelines, perhaps they had noticed Gina's death stare too. I skated past them as gracefully as I could, and then felt a whoosh of air as Murdock circled around me.

"Little Anya," he said in his dark voice, "you're not much of a Mer."

My eyes widened. For him to be so careless and flippant about calling me a Mer in public was odd. There was no one close enough to overhear, but Gina was not far away.

Had I been wrong with my senses? Did she already know about us? Had Merrick told her?

Suddenly, I wondered whether Merrick would have accepted her as a mate since they seemed so drawn to one another. My grandmother had found herself a human mate and sought out the match regardless of parental approval. *Maybe Merrick wasn't strong enough to do the same?*

"Well luckily for you, I'm not your mate." I

answered.

His look was disapproving, but I continued to skate until he stopped in front of me, forcing me to stop as well.

"You know, he doesn't want you, he wants her. Merrick only picked you to bide his time."

A sharp pain tore through me. Merrick had been honest. He did tell me he had picked me because he wanted more time, had encouraged me to date others since we would spend our lives together and I had believed him, naively. Perhaps he had no intention of ever being with me. His actions had seemed different, but now watching him as he skated and looked at Gina I could tell there was emotion there. I didn't use my power over him, but I reached out to feel what he felt, and it was as I suspected. He cared for her, maybe it was more than he felt towards me.

"Yeah I know," I said to Murdock, my face hiding my emotions trembling beneath the surface. I willed them away. I didn't want him to think he had even the slightest victory over me. "Want to move out of my way?" I asked my eyes darkening, "I'm thirsty." He stared at me, scrutinizing to the point where it felt like we had been standing there for far too long.

"See anything you like?" I asked, my voice more acrid than I had intended. He scowled and skated back to his group. Merrick who was at Gina's side looked at me softly, but I didn't let his handsome face weaken my anger.

I skated off to the hot cocoa stand looking for Evelyn and Leah. I had spotted them and was about to make my way over to their table when a hot sting seared my skin. I grabbed my side as pain rippled over it, trying not to buckle. Luckily, the people around me were preoccupied with their hot chocolate and conversing, they hadn't noticed my pained expression.

I shuffled around to the other side of the stand and unzipped my jacket to check my skin. Blue, purple, and red scales were dotting my sides, I had finally begun scaling, and of course, at the very worst time.

"Dammit," I muttered under my breath. I shuffled back to the ice skating over to the stands where I kept my shoes. My movements were hurried, frantic, as the pain came in stronger waves. My scales were spreading and I needed to submerge myself in water, the sooner, the better.

I tore off my skates as fast as they would allow and pulled on my boots. Another patch of scales spread and I hissed lowly. Returning the skates quickly to the rental stand, I walked towards the entrance of the park. Even if I called my parents they wouldn't answer. They were in the lab and they usually turned off their cell phones when there. I called my parents anyway and left a voicemail. If I was lucky, they might check and pick me up along the way home. I wanted to call a cab, but I didn't have enough money. I couldn't really tell Evelyn or Leah what was going on, and they planned to stay until the ice carving and light show that night. My only option was to walk, and even though it would take hours I would need to do it as best I could. I just prayed the scaling didn't reach my face or hands before that time.

"Anya," A voice behind me spoke.

I turned to see Merrick. His eyes scanned me quickly and then fixated on my arm wrapped around my side.

"You're scaling?" He half-asked, half-stated with concern lined on his face.

"Apparently I'm becoming an actual Mermaid," I said. "Bad news for you I guess."

"You need to get home." He said.

"You think genius?" I asked with furrowed

brows.

"You're being sarcastic with me?" He looked wounded and then reached for my shoulder. "Let me take you home."

I pulled away from him.

"Ummm, I think thy Royal Highness, Gina, might object, Prince Merrick."

He laughed, a completely warm and wave crashing laugh that fluttered all over me and made me blush when his eyes locked on mine with affection.

"What does that make you?" He asked pulling off his gloves and shoving them into his pocket, then picking up a handful of snow, and glancing around us. He lifted my jacket and placed a warm, wet hand over my scales. Immediately it soothed the burning sensation. I looked up at him, feeling dazed. I couldn't believe that I had let him lift my jacket. I couldn't believe I had let him touch me. He was very close, so close that if he bent slightly, his lips would brush my forehead. He was touching me. His warm hand pressed firmly on my stomach.

"The court jester," I replied regaining my wit.

He shook his head and his hand left my skin and bent to pick up more snow.

"For that, I'm going to have to start calling you Princess," he said, his tone slightly authoritative.

He moved to return to me but a shrill call stopped him.

"Merrick! There you are!"

Gina ran up to his side and wrapped herself around his arm, pulling him over to her.

"I was looking for you." She said with a sexy high gloss pout, even bundled up in winter clothes she still managed to look great wearing a short woollen jacket and tights with a mini-skirt. She was always wearing mini-skirts.

Didn't she own a pair of pants?

"What are you doing all the way over here anyway, you're missing everything *important*." Her eyes were like daggers when she glanced at me.

"I'm going to take Anya home, she's not feeling well."

"She looks fine to me." She said, her stare still cold. I was about to open my mouth to confirm that I was fine, but the scales spread again, and my breath hitched, making me tense. She noticed the change in my appearance.

"You're not going to puke are you?" She asked with plenty of disgust at the notion. "Fine, take her home I guess, but give me a goodbye kiss." She said hanging off the lapels of his coat.

My stomach actually started to churn at that thought, and Merrick looked at me uncomfortable before he bent and brushed his lips to hers, his neck tense. Rather than a sweet kiss, Gina turned it into something monstrous with her tongue wrestling in Merrick's mouth. Disgusted, I turned away unable to look at him, at them.

"Bye, Anna!" She called out to me, and I flailed an arm out in a wave goodbye glancing back at her. She loved to call me anything, but my actual name. I wanted to give Merrick a death stare, but I couldn't even bring myself to look at him.

"I'm going home." I said beginning to leave. He grabbed my shoulders and pulled me back to him, into him. So I shut my eyes, looking down. The truth was, I should be furious with him, for flirting with me when he wanted her, for kissing her in front of me when I was betrothed to him, but instead my body wanted to lean against him and be comforted.

"Anya, I'm sorry about that," he said, the words tender.

"Just take me home." I said pinching my eyes tighter.

"Will you open your eyes?" He asked.

I shook my head no. "I can't look at you right now." If I did, I was afraid tears would be streaming down my face. I turned away from him, opening my eyes and walking briskly towards the parking lot. He let out a deep sigh and walked behind me. With every third or fourth step my breath caught as a tremor caused my scales to spread.

"How exactly are you taking me home?" I asked, as the thought dawned on me.

"My ATV is over there." He said pointing to it hidden between some trees.

"Oh," I replied, a little astonished that he had ridden it out here. Then again snow, ice, or rain were things that wielded to most Mers. There was no danger there. He picked up more snow as we walked.

"You should soak the scales again," he said moving closer to me as if to complete the task himself. I hopped two feet away from him bending down for snow of my own, which I hastily stuffed under my coat and clothing, shuddering at the sudden chill.

"I got it! All set to go," I said grabbing the helmet he handed me. I slapped it on and finally looked him square in the eye. He had a pained expression on his face.

"You're going to have to hold onto me, Anya," his words almost apologetic.

"That's fine." I said terse, wishing that he would stop saying my name in such an intimately lyrical way. The scales spread to my buttocks and I jumped, yelping in pain. So I shifted, letting some of the snow drip down over them. "Can we get a move on it?" I asked gritting my teeth. For a moment, I wondered if he had anticipated our first tense moments.

He nodded and fired the engine up. I climbed on wrapping my arms around his waist. I was actually thankful for the distracting feel of me hugging him. The scales spread out a few more times along the ride, and sweat broke out on my upper lip and along my spine. By the time we arrived at my house I was exhausted, emotionally and physically. I jumped off the four-wheeler as soon as he cut the engine, and pulled off the helmet quickly tossing it to him.

"Thanks," I said ready to turn and run into the house, "I owe you one."

He flipped up the visor on the helmet. "Anya wait, about what Murdock said..." But I couldn't wait, I was in pain, and angry, and sad. I couldn't deal with him and Gina right now, not with my body in the middle of a huge change. I ran quickly up the porch and into the house, not even bothering to lock the door behind me and stripped off my clothes while I made my way to the bathroom.

I turned the spout on full blast and soaked myself underneath the shower. Immediately, I felt relief. The water splashing down on me was so soothing. Finally, I felt the water washing the pain away. I stayed that way, with my forehead against the tiles, for a good ten minutes before I realized I needed to move. For the first time I got to take a good look at my scales. I had seen other Mer scales before, my parents' scales were both red, and most Mers were a mixture of green and blue. Yet mine were none of those colours. At first, they seemed to be all three colours, but the more I looked at them the more I realized the base of the scale was purple— that was odd.

My parents came home half an hour later and discovered me still soaking in the bathtub. By that time the scales had spread all over, but were now slowly retreating, making swirling patterns in a sheen against my skin.

"Oh my poor little one," she said to me crouching against the side of the tub. She brushed aside my wet hair, her eyes filled with sorrow. "Your father and I feel terrible that we weren't there for you when the transformation started. We came as soon as we got the message. Are you alright?"

"Mmmhmmm," I mumbled softly, my eyes closed in rest. "I am fine, Mom." My tail swished down and sank into the water slowly.

"We should have been here," she said scowling.

"I forgive you." I said wanting her to let go of her guilt. I heard a light rap at the door. My father opened it only a smidgen, enough so that he could speak through the crack.

"How are you Tiger Shark?" He asked with the same sadness in his voice.

"I'm fine Dad, really, you two shouldn't feel so sad." Mers were terrible for feeling guilty, especially when they felt they had failed a loved one.

"I promise I won't come in sweetheart, but your mother and I are truly sorry."

"Just buy me a big chocolate cake," I said jokingly, but really wanting to stuff my face with some. The combination of the physical pain and emotional trauma had me desperately seeking the comfort of sugary food.

"I'm on it," he said in a serious tone and closed the door. I could hear the jingle of keys and I knew he had left the house for the cake.

"Oh we need more Perrier too," my mother suddenly realized, "be right back love."

HALF AN HOUR AFTER that, once my tail had dissipated back into my humanoid legs, I was seated at the kitchen table, slowly shovelling chocolate cake into my mouth. The rich cocoa was decadent on my tongue. I was tired, far more tired than I had expected to be.

"You need your rest Anya," My mother said watching my lids droop, "the change that took the place is only the beginning, it's the first major trigger towards your transformation and you can expect many more changes in the weeks to come."

I already knew what she was telling me. I had read all the books on my transformation. I had asked dozens of questions on when I would change and why it was taking so long. I had prepared myself for the shift two years earlier since most Mer's scale just before the age of twelve. Now that it had happened, I felt unprepared. After two years of no signs, I had feared that it would never even take place.

Yet, here it was--my transcendence. Of course, after I had finally found a mate, one who didn't want me, would I begin to transform into something else. I felt no different though. I was still the same person with my similarly neurotic thoughts. I hadn't instantly grown long shiny hair and filled out. All of a sudden I didn't want to change. I wanted to stay as the same me I had been all along. I glanced in the nearby mirror and realized, I had been beautiful all along, and becoming a Mer had nothing to do with it.

"I'm going to bed." I said plopping my dish and fork into the sink.

My parents didn't even protest that I had left a dirty dish there as they watched me walk up the stairs.

"Get some rest honey," my mom called to me.

"Sleep well," my dad echoed.

I nodded my head and then added cheekily, "yeah...hold my calls, will you?"

Chapter 15

I WOKE UP THE NEXT morning jerking forward with the feeling that I was falling. It was that treacherous feeling of being so close to the edge of something and then tumbling down before you could stop yourself. My heart was pounding.

"Are you okay?" I heard from my window seat. I looked up to see Merrick getting up and making his way over to me.

Was I dreaming? I pinched myself hard on my arm and he sat beside me and rubbed my reddened skin.

"You're not dreaming Anya." He said, his voice falling over me like cool silk. I shuddered and he pulled the blankets up around me. "Our parents all got called into Halifax because of some glitch in the big project they're working on. They didn't want to leave you alone so soon after scaling."

"Oh." I said softly.

"Rayne, Pearl, and Coral wanted to come over,

but I figured it would be good for us to talk."

"Yeah I guess so," I said not wanting to admit to myself that we desperately needed to talk.

"Here, you should drink some water," he said handing me a glass. "You need to hydrate." I drained the contents of it and placed the empty cup back on my nightstand. Merrick got up for a moment and riffled through his carrier bag left by on the window seat. He pulled out a small plastic container.

"You'll want to use this." He said as he wiggled it in his hand. He returned to me, and sat on the bed, only this time he was much closer.

"Give me your arm," he said twisting off the cap letting a strongly herbed smelling scent waft into the air. I could tell there was seaweed in the concoction that looked like a thick cream.

Hesitantly, I removed my left arm from beneath the blanket and lifted it towards him. He warmed some of the spread in his palms before rubbing it onto my skin and as he massaged it felt delightful. I wanted to collapse again in relaxation. My eyes grew droopy enjoying the pressure of his touch.

"You must not talk about me with your parents much," he said suddenly grabbing some more of the cream and rubbing it in.

"What makes you say that?"

"Well, they let me come over here and stay with you."

"Yeah and..."

"Well that must mean that you haven't told them what a jerk I am."

I let his comment sink in, wondering what had brought that out.

"Are you a jerk?" I asked.

"You know what I mean. Sometimes I can be."

"What makes you say that?"

He rubbed his neck. "I guess, I neglect you at school, and Gina. There's Gina."

I frowned.

"You're not a jerk. Gina is mostly."

His eyes intensified while looking at me as though he was agreeing.

I shrugged. "I guess that makes you a jerk by association, Loverboy"

He looked at me confused. "You weren't supposed to say that."

"No?" I asked with my eyebrow arched quizzically. "What was I supposed to say?" I asked in playful whisper.

"That's all wrong." He said, a thought-filled look on his face like he was deciphering a complex mathematical equation.

I shrugged. "What can you do?" And then offered him my other arm, I was taking full advantage of a doting Merrick while I could. He rubbed absentmindedly.

"I saw…" he began and trailed off staring off into space.

"Saw?" I asked. "What do you mean you saw?"

He didn't answer my question.

"Nothing just… Has Zale spoken to you at all?"

"Lately?" I asked. "No. Actually, I don't think we've ever spoken. Maybe once, back in November." There was that dream I had, but that didn't count. I wasn't about to tell him about it and sound all crazy.

"He said he would speak to you." He looked at me more sternly, as though I were lying.

"He hasn't spoken to me, Merrick. I'm sorry. I don't really know why your brother needs to talk to me, but he hasn't since before my birthday. Isn't he in Atlantis anyway?"

"He argued with me about it for hours. I begged

him not to, but he said you deserved to know."

"Know what?" I said suddenly wondering if I really was dreaming again.

"Nothing."

"Nothing?" I asked annoyed. "Alright fine, don't tell me, but at least tell me what was supposed to happen twenty seconds ago."

He was silent for a moment, still rubbing the cream in before a mischievous smile crept up on his mouth,

"Merrick."

He sighed. "You were supposed to say 'You're not a jerk, but you could always be nicer to me.'"

"Oh really? I think what I said was far more interesting. That sounds boring."

"Well, then I was supposed to kiss you." He looked up at me, his teal eyes intoxicating.

My stomach fluttered at the mere thought, but I couldn't help, but scowl thinking about the first time Merrick had kissed me, and then the confusing dream with Zale.

"What is it with you Price boys and kissing me?" I muttered.

"What?" Merrick asked as he jerked back and his face darkened. His eyebrows knit with anger.

"Oh no. That's not what I meant..." I began with my hand held out.

"You meant that Zale kissed you!"

"No! NO! He didn't! I promise you he didn't. It was just some weird dream I had around my birthday."

"That's even worse!" He shouted, "He's being sneaky!"

"Why are you so mad?" I asked reaching out to touch his hand. "It was a dream Merrick." I stared at him while his jaw tensed. He didn't look at me, shook his head in disapproval.

He finally spoke through gritted teeth. "Because you're my mate, and he knows it." A lesser Mer would have shouted at him that he had kissed Gina, and stormed out of the room in a fit, but I was not that Mer. Instead I chose my words carefully.

"You're not being fair. It was a dream Merrick. It's not like you had to witness his tongue in my mouth. It was a peck, in a dream." I was his? He used the word 'my' yet definitely didn't seem very possessive of me.

His eyes shot back to mine with a pained expression. "I'm sorry, Anya." He said softly. "I really am. It's just that... Oh how do I explain to you what it is I feel..."

"It's fine." I said, still annoyed but too tired to argue. I gave him the arm he had not finished. He resumed with the lotion.

"What else happened in the dream Anya?"

I sighed, not really want to seem fanciful, but it wouldn't hurt to tell him. "He told me that he could teleport through water, and that he could see into the future, especially when someone was faced with a choice, and he gave me the e-reader that you two bought me for my birthday, which by the way you never told me if you ever read that thank you letter I wrote you."

He had nodded as I spoke considering each thing. "I read it. It was appreciated. What else Anya?"

"That's it." There was no way I was telling him that Zale had told me Merrick loved me, and that he himself loved me. That would just open another can of worms that I preferred to leave on the shelf, and possibly in a dimly lit corner.

"That's it?" He didn't look very convinced.

"Oh and he said he needed my help, which I

promised to provide." Why I was telling Merrick all of this, I didn't know. I felt that it was partly the guilt of knowing that it hurt him to hear that Zale has kissed me in a dream. It was as if it affected him more so than it hurt me to see him with Gina. There was rage and pain rumbling beneath the surface of his exterior.

"Alright so he did speak with you through a dream," he said in realization.

"He can do that?"

"Yes." Merrick nodded and then it was as if he released all of the darkness he was carrying. "Its fine that he kissed you. I'll deal with it later. Are you going to give me your bare legs now?" He asked grabbing more of the cream.

I suddenly remembered that I had taken my pants off when I had jumped into bed the night before and was now only wearing my tee shirt a pair of boxer short underwear with a pattern of little Christmas boxes on them.

"How do you know my legs are bare?"

"I told you I saw this happening differently."

"*You* saw it? Not you too!" I asked my voice embarking on a higher pitch. He looked at where my legs would be underneath the covers and I shivered a bit from the intensity of his eyes.

"Yes Anya, I saw it *through* Zale, he shared the vision. So..." He glanced at my legs again looking a little too eager.

"You want me to just be a hussy, don't you?"

He laughed a deep and rich laugh.

"What exactly happened Merrick? In the version of what you saw." I eyed him suspiciously.

He looked away from me, trying to contain his amusement at my questioning.

"We kissed."

"That's it?" Now it was my turn to ask.

"A lot," he admitted. "Maybe for hours, I dunno."

"Hours..." I whispered, starting to picture the image mentally. I shifted in the bed feeling a blush overtake my face.

"Your human side is coming out," he said with a wink, "Mers are never this modest." He sighed. "You're going to have to give me those legs of yours miss, my hands are already covered." I opened my mouth to protest, but nothing came out so he continued.

"Don't worry, you'll like it." He wiggled his eyebrows. I wanted to giggle, because of his sudden comical display, but stopped myself. He was right. If I was more like a Mer I'd be looking for ways to entice him, not holding back.

"Don't laugh," I said. I had decent thighs considering the rest of me was too small, but my calves were slender.

"I won't." He replied.

Thankfully he started with my ankles. I think I would have gone into shock if he had touched my thighs right away. He knew I was nervous so he worked his way up each leg a little at a time making sure they were equal, when he got to my knees I realized I was a goner.

He was gentle with my thighs, but by that point I was all hot and bothered and I couldn't take anymore. It felt too intimate with him being here in my room, with how he was caring for me. He had barely rubbed a little bit of the salve on before he went to get more cream, when I lost it.

"Merrick stop!" I cried out. He paused immediately and his eyes hesitated. I flung myself back on the bed in relief when he didn't continue. He closed the jar instead and lay down beside me. His head propped up by his arm.

"You're too tense Anya."

I bit my lip, purposely not looking at him. So he titled my face in his direction.

"You know I won't hurt you, right? I'd never make you do anything you don't want."

I looked into his eyes, into the depth of them swirling beautifully and felt comforted. He would never hurt me. He couldn't harm me and I trusted him.

"I know." I responded softly. Then I did what I should have done earlier, I leaned forward and kissed him. Being close to him felt right, and that was what made me most nervous. I didn't know if I would be able to keep resisting him, giving him the space that he seemed to want.

He deepened the kiss so slightly, so softly and then pulled me into his arms into an embrace. We lay like that for a little while, with me nestled into his side and him sneaking occasional kisses. Kisses that I hadn't expected him to want.

"How can you kiss me when you're dating her?" I finally asked my finger running along his forearm.

He smiled at me, his eyes incredible and intoxicating. "Because, I'm a jerk," he said and then he hugged me tighter, letting out a deep sigh.

Chapter 16

By the time the school week had started, I had regained my strength. The scaling had been a quick process despite being draining, and I was better at controlling the pace of my transformation once my skin hit water. For most Mers this was the challenging part, learning to control the Mer essence within you was important. Otherwise, the moment you hit water, it was intuitive to change- no matter where you were. That impulse needed to be mastered. Our secrets needed to be protected.

The first couple of times I had bathed I stared in awe at my tail. My mother had been amazed by the colour of my scales. She had never seen a tail like mine, which was mauve. The end of my tail was translucent with a lavender iridescent sheen and quite wispy.

Lately, when not testing myself by washing my hands or going for a bath. I had been e-mailing Coral and spending my spare time with Pearl in the school library. I had told her about the Mer incantation for water boiling that I had finally managed to interpret from the *grimoire* and we decided that the upcoming weekend we would test it out. She and Coral had been missing Rayne a lot since she had left early for college and had invited me to join them skating on Thursday night. It would be the perfect opportunity to heat some water for cocoa after at their house and I couldn't wait.

Ondine had offered to drop us off at the lake. She and Caspian had actually finished their work a night early and were resting at home after a busy week of orders from the mid-ocean. I was surprised when my own parents had even called me to let me know they would pick me up from the Price home later on their way back from town.

As soon as we arrived at the lake, we found Murdock and Hurley there sitting down on a bench not far from the snowy shoreline. Maybe he was here to see Coral, but something about his presence had me feeling uneasy. I was tempted to ask the girls if they wanted to go somewhere else, but Ondine had already left us. I followed Coral and Pearl to the makeshift rink bench set up and we sat down to remove our shoes. The silence of our focusing was quickly interrupted.

"Coral."

"Coral."

"Coooorall!" Murdock spoke loudly from where he and Hurley sat.

"WHAT!" She said, and snapped her neck to his direction.

"Why don't you come say hi to me?" He made a sad pouting face. When I looked at Pearl, I could tell she was thinking the same thing I was... clearly, he was playing some game.

"What do you want Murdock?" Coral asked, her voice sounding annoyed.

"What do you think I want?" He asked throwing a snowball in our direction which luckily fell short.

"Nothing good." Coral muttered under her breath.

"I WANT MY BETROTHED TO COME HERE AND GREET ME PROPERLY." He demanded.

"No! Don't speak to me that way either!"

"No!?" He said. "Don't you dare say no to me Coral! Get. Over. Here. Now!"

Pearl looked at me with frown, her lips thinning with displeasure. She didn't like the way he was treating her sister either.

I looked at Coral and then sent a wave of strength to her, which helped relieved some of the tension in her shoulders.

"Come on," she said, "let's skate."

We all moved eagerly towards the middle and began swirling and twirling around, trying to mimic figure skaters. From the trees I could hear the sound of a motor rumbling and a few moments later the engine of an ATV was cut. I looked up to see Merrick removed his helmet. He was alone and walked over to meet with Murdock and Hurley who were snickering about something I had no mind to listen to.

"Your sister sucks as a mate!" Murdock said as Merrick approached.

Merrick shook his head. "Saying stuff like that is definitely the best way to win her over too." I smiled at him as I completed my lap and his eyes caught mine as he pushed back his dark hair from his eyes,

"Watch this," Murdock said.

"Coral."

"Coral."

"Coral."

"COOORALL!" Murdock threw his head back as he belted her name out one last time. Behind me, a few metres back on the frozen river. Coral and Pearl skated to a stop and we all eyed him. How obnoxious! I had enough, he had only said a few things, but I was past the point of annoyed for my friend.

"Why don't you can it Murdock! You're worse than a squawking seagull."

"What did you say to me!?" He asked shooting up from the bench and moving a few feet closer to the ice.

Merrick was behind him, and he looked like he was ready to pounce should Murdock move closer to me.

"That's close enough, Murdock." Merrick said in a low growl.

"Your little mate, Merrick, shouldn't be talking to me like that." He looked back at Merrick and then to me again. I rolled my eyes.

"Leave her alone," Coral said, she and Pearl still standing still on the ice behind me.

"Leave her alone." Murdock repeated in a whiny voice. "Baby, of course I'll leave little Anya be."

He looked from Coral to Hurley and suddenly I had that same gut wrenching feeling like on the day I had scaled. Hurley's hand shot up and the ice beneath me gave way. The cold water was biting as it sliced into my legs and I held onto the edge. I fought the change, trying to scramble back up on the ice, but it was no use I was slipping.

"She has no powers!" Merrick roared, pushing him out of the way. He ran towards me while Coral and Pearl tried to skate close enough without falling in, they had leaned down closer to the surface, but weakened from what Hurley had done with his powers, the gap was widening fast.

Everything was happening so quickly. I could feel both Merrick and Pearl tug at me with their powers trying to get the water to keep me up above the surface, but it wasn't working, they were too frantic. With the strength of the current I was sucked under the ice, sinking down into the chill. Now was not the time to change, though, anyone could show up at any minute . The last thing that I needed was to be seen in broad daylight with a tail. The clunky skates were weighing me down, but I fought the weight of them and began swimming to the surface. Somewhere near the opening I saw Merrick dive beneath the water and he was quickly swimming towards me. In seconds he had my arms and he pulled us down to gain momentum before quickly shooting up breaking the thick ice surface above us. His hand pushed the water up, and we jetted from the force of it behind us, onto the edge of the river where the ice was still solid. Merrick held me close to him while my teeth chattered. His free hand wiped away my wet hair.

"You didn't change?" he asked me looking at my legs.

"I tr-tri-tri-tried n-no-not tto." I said.

Soon, everyone was gathered around us, Murdock was hanging back a few feet. Merrick's eyes, like daggers, were fixed on him.

"You said she changed, Coral." He confessed sounding displeased with himself.

"She hasn't gotten her powers yet." Merrick said, his arms wrapping tighter around me. "You're lucky my mate is between us otherwise both of you would be at the bottom of that lake right now.

"That doesn't make any sense." Hurley said also looking ashamed.

"I'mmm, I'mmmm one qu qu.." Merrick placed his fingers over my chattering lips to stop my explanation, his eyes were so apologetic.

"She's one quarter human." He said looking at them challengingly. "What was that Hurley? What if it was your mate?"

Hurley rubbed his neck. Merrick's jaw ticked, he was angry. I'd never witnessed him this upset.

Hurley's head fell. "I'm sorry, I... I..." I raised my hand for him to stop. Obviously, he thought it would be a funny joke. Both of them did.

"Me too," Murdock added, and I could have died from shock.

"It's not okay," Merrick started, "not yet, but Murdock, you better get on this," he spoke gesturing to the both of us. Murdock shook his head, snapping out of the stunned response he had and pulled up his sleeve. As his hand stretched out the water began to heat up and evaporate from us.

"Ouch!" I winced.

"It stings a little," Murdock said sheepishly, but I was at least grateful he had agreed to dry us. Fifteen minutes later, when we were both dry, I slipped out of Merrick's arms and was met with hugs by both Coral and Pearl.

"Anyone up for hot chocolate?" I asked them looking up towards the piles of wavy hair on top of my head. There was no use in being emotional right now. I was alright. Everyone was okay.

"Definitely!" Pearl and Coral said in unison.

We all decided to go back to the Price home, and before I knew it I was once again riding on the back of Merrick's ATV. My arms were wrapped around him, only this time there wasn't any pain. Coral had, of course, gone with Murdock, after she had swatted him across his back a few times for teasing her that he'd be reckless. Apparently, he didn't know how to learn a lesson. And Pearl had agreed to ride with Hurley after he had made profuse promises that they would both arrive at our destination in one piece.

I had anticipated the drive to be slightly awkward between Merrick and me. He had held me in his arms, while Murdock dried us for what had probably felt a bit too long, but he hadn't gestured for me to get out of them. A few times we had both shifted around to dry faster in certain spots, but we remained together and he didn't push me away so I stayed neatly tucked against him. Now that we were riding back to his home, I felt connected to him, grateful for his presence. He had protected me the way he swore that he would.

We pulled into the driveway long after the others had, and I was not surprised to see they had already gone inside. Part of me wondered if he had done it on purpose. Driven slowly to give us more time together, and I wouldn't know unless I asked him. So as I slowly removed my helmet, standing beside a still seated, Merrick, I blurted out my question.

"Just had to spend a few extra minutes alone with me, eh? Couldn't drive just a little faster?"

His eyes looked up from his helmet, surprised, without the time to be composed. There was something else beneath the grin that broke out. I surmised it might be satisfaction.

"I haven't the faintest idea what you mean, Miss Anya," he replied in a way that seemed oddly softened. When he looked into my eyes there was a moment when I thought he might say how he felt and I wondered what he saw in me then. I wondered what he was thinking, if my words had incited anything from his heart.

I wanted to kiss him, to walk over and toss his helmet aside, and plant one square on his lips. I think he knew, because he watched me quickly lick my lips, with an odd look of hope.

"Guess we should go make hot chocolate then, eh?" he said in the same child-like soft voice.

I moved closer to him, the soft crunch of my jacket noisy while I hugged him.

"I'm grateful you were there to help, Merrick." My blood rushed into my cheeks and pounded into my ears before the fear gave way to joy and comfort, and then the wonderful feeling of his breath against my face as I pulled away from him. He wrapped his arms around my waist and holding me then, it felt right, like we were complete.

"I don't ever want to lose you, Anya."

I didn't want to ruin the moment, but I had to be honest with him. We weren't together, his words were those of a boyfriend, a love, but that was not what he wanted. I wasn't even sure what I wanted. "Merrick, we're not really..."

"That doesn't matter," he interrupted. "None of *that* does..."

"Oh?" I said, my smile waning into a firm question.

"What matters is this moment. I need you to understand, that I mean it when I say I never want to lose you. I will always do everything in my power to protect you."

"Merrick..." I tried to protest, to reassure him that he owed me nothing, that I understood his need for freedom because I sometimes craved it just as much.

His hand pressed firmly against mine, "I want you to remember that. No matter what else happens between us. I respect our parents' contract. It means something to me."

You mean something to me was the only thing he didn't say.

Chapter 17

I was watching the snow melt. It had been weeks, almost a month since I had last spent time with Merrick. After all of us had gone to the Prices' for hot chocolate; the day had been slow, relaxing like a day you spend in pyjamas with a hot cup of tea.

We'd sat down to watch a few movies, and then before I knew it the sleepiness of night had crept in and we had all gone our separate ways.

I had come home and retreated to the dark coziness of my room. A few candles lit while I read through the Mer *grimoire* that Mrs. Keller had given me. I was learning of the enchantments and runes. It was then that I realized that this book had to have been given to me for a reason, and at the time it had felt like perhaps it was to break the bond.

Maybe Merrick was right and we were wasting our time with the contract that our parents had sewn magically. I started reading, thinking that there had to be a way we could free ourselves, or at least that I could free him so that he could be what he wanted. Even in the moments we had shared together, I still felt as though he was holding something back.

Now, I was in the same spot as I had been then, perched on my window seat with my eyes glancing out of the window. Only it was bright; the white of outside stark and harsh against my eyes instead of shadowed mounds of snow. Water was dripping down off the icicles on the trees; they were clear daggers of beauty. I wondered what the spring would bring. The winter had been playful, but serious. I'd met my mate and finally scaled. *Would the spring slow my constant changes and bring about the baking heat I dreaded from the summertime; or would it be different here, calmer, with a inspiring breeze?*

Soon the flowers would be here, and even though something about the way the earth changed was hopeful, I felt uneasy about the weeks ahead. I had skipped the Valentine's Day dance the weekend after my time with Merrick at the pond. Too much had happened in January for me to witness Gina and Merrick together on the dance floor.

Instead, I had spent February learning the charms of rocks and stones. Water gems and their properties as per the *grimoire* laying in my lap. It wasn't all studious though. I had still been taking time to visit Mrs Keller on occasion for discussions over tea, and the chance to look at her old photo albums and hear her stories. Cookies too, despite the massive Christmas cookie exchange. There were always lots of treats for us to share together.

With some resources from some of my parent's colleagues, I was able to decipher the older inscriptions in the book. I had slowly made a project of cataloguing pages of the information and transcripts. The old leathery pages of the book made a thick flapping sound as I turned the pages. Each sheet was slowly slicing the air.

Today, I had finally got to the page about fish bone reading. A lot of the first few pages in the book were light hearted in their magical approach. There were some beauty enchantment spells like the *Albayrous* one that Coral had attempted to complete for me, and the enchantment one that Rayne had mastered for her shampoo. These kinds of spells were lesser in their magical pull. They were the kind of thing easily passed down in oral history or in small community meetings. Then there was the water evaporation one which was the first spell requiring some actual skill. I had a small amount of luck with it, but I knew that it would take lots of time for my confidence to grow. It involved a lot of concentration, so much so, that when I had tried it a week earlier, I had only successfully evaporated one droplet. I had a huge migraine after and spent the rest of the day sleeping it off.

I flipped the book open to the fish bone readings. They were next in the book, five full pages of details followed by the letters of the moon, which was an impressive ten page spread. Yet these were only skimming the surface, I was pages and pages away from the hero page, from the time changing enchantment. I had been discouraged at first by my lack of progress with the water evaporation. For days I had thought of giving up. Until, I learned to accept that there were other things in the book that may have been better suited to my skills. As I read, I learned that bone readings weren't easy. They were better suited to Mers with empathy or kin skills like Rayne. It was enough to spark some hope in me.

The bones of a fish could point to different paths or choices, the magic of it would reveal things that could not been seen with the eye, or known by the person asking the question. If properly treated, they could be ground down and scattered over water after many readings and their powers seemed to wane. This kind of reading would be powerful, but needed a specific question in mind. I had to rub the fish bones with an anointed object wrapped in arrowhead plant leaves. The object was most powerful if it was a river or ocean stone. There were a few drawings of some with the right kind of minerals or textures commonly found near certain bodies of water. Then, there was an incantation to read:

Fal'rae brin diu al fae rah päer

I had to place one of the bones at the end of a cloth, or piece of paper if you wanted to keep the reading. Then pour boiling water over the bone and watch the answers spread out onto the medium.
 I wanted to do the reading soon, so I devised a plan to get my supplies on the weekend. I needed some answers about Merrick and Zale and I felt like this would point me in the right direction.

Chapter 18

THE MOON WAS MISSING tonight in the sky over the cove. My Mer eyes were enhanced enough for me to see everything, but I had a flashlight to help better distinguish the colours in the night. Water was shimmering, little flickers glistening, as the waves rolled in and swept softly against the sand. The breeze was an inspiring flutter against my cheeks. Standing there seemed solitary and lonesome, dangerous almost, but I felt as though that moment had filled me with warmth and peace.

    I would sometimes sit in my room and meditate about this haven-like place. I knew that it must exist somewhere, though I wasn't quite sure how or where I might find it. In reading the *grimoire* I had learned new things about Mers and their abilities to sense water.

    With my empathic powers growing I was starting to realize how my emotions linked to my environment. I had dreamed of this place so many times before that I had started to sense it out. In the weeks prior whenever I went for drives with my parents I looked for signs of it until one day there it was. Not that far from where I lived, the secret cove was only about a seven minute walk. It was off a long stretch of rocky shore that curved out until it ducked around a corner and into a grassy beach front surrounding a circle of water. A few large rocks seemed to be marking an unofficial entrance. I was searching for what I knew must be there, the rock I needed for my reading. It was late, I was out of the house later than I should have been, but for the first time I felt determined to get some answers.

    My parents were sleeping pretty soundly when I left from the back entrance off the kitchen. The project they were working on in the lab had been keeping them so busy lately, it was a wonder they had slept at all. More often, in the past few weeks they had burned the midnight oil, only one of them returning home to spend the night with me before joining the other at the base camp in the morning. Then they would switch off and repeat the same pattern again. I was starting to worry about their health. They were overworked.

    The flashlight darted around the ground until at last I spotted the rock! Black and shimmering it had been smoothed over time with specks of minerals catching the light. I reached down to grab it and placed it in my pocket when I heard a noise behind me and turned quickly, suddenly very scared.

    "It's just me Anya."

    How he found me I wasn't sure, he reached his hand out to mine helping me step over a large rock and I felt complete disbelief. Merrick had found this cove. My heart calmed from its sheer panic at the thought of a stranger finding me here.

"This place is beautiful" he said as I stepped down and closer to him. He turned to watch the water against the shore.

"Merrick I never expected to see you here. It's late."

"Something in your heart must have called me then."

"What makes you think it was my heart?"

"Well I'd like to think that I'm in there somewhere."

"Oh? — Why is that? Would you say that I'm in yours?"

"Of course you are. Our bond made it so."

"Right."

I watched the water until my eyes travelled up to the stars dotting the darkened sky. Again his words left me wanting more from him. I wished that for once her would tell me how he honestly felt, no bonding spell or magic – just him.

Even though we had spent days together that were pleasant, fun even, I couldn't help but feel like maybe this mating with me wasn't really what he had wanted.

"You've gone quiet Anya."

"I've nothing more to add really, you've summed it all so well."

"Have I though?"

"Yes, Merrick, you have." I clenched the stone tighter in my pocket.

Maybe for now I would have to leave things the way they were, but I was learning more and more every day. For all I knew there could be a bond breaking spell in the *grimoire*.

Our parents knew what they were doing with that contract. All Mers did. And now we seemed to be stuck together forever like tangled seaweeds. *How did*

I feel for him? I felt muddled. Perhaps the moon cycle had something to do with it, a waning moon was always a vulnerable time for us Mer folk, the new moon was even worse. Merrick stepped closer to the water.

"Want to take a dip?" he asked.

I had already seen this moment what felt like a million times before. Only this night wasn't a full moon, and it seemed all wrong. There were no waves rolling in. The water instead pitch black and still. It was eerie. I shook my head no.

"I'll walk you home then," he said wrapping an arm around my shoulders.

As we walked, the silence was awkward, until at last he said something.

"Zale mentioned this to me," he finally admitted, though he still didn't tell me anything else. I didn't bother asking why, obviously this moment had something to do with a choice. I just wasn't sure if it was his or mine.

THE NEXT MORNING, I woke feeling like maybe I had dreamed the previous night. Until, I looked at my bedside table and noticed the rock wrapped in arrowhead leaves. Then, I recalled the fish bones I'd also saved from the previous night's dinner. I grabbed them all eagerly, tearing a piece of parchment from my sketchbook and running down the stairs. After I poured the water into a small bowl, I arranged the paper with the bone at the edge of it closest to me. I tapped my fingers on the countertop to intensify my water boiling chant until steam slowly wafted up from the surface of the water.

I poured it, slowly, focusing on my question in my mind. As the water ran over the bone it met the page and thick black lines appeared beneath the surface of the bone and spreading onto the paper, like ink it was seeping over the surface in a wave of motion and spreading out. At first I had felt like the bone had not properly understood my question. The lines were spreading out like the limbs of a coral reef, but then the words began to appear, in *Mercrutian* and with so many different meanings like the words for choice or freedom or love. Thin and wisp-like they glinted in the light. Some were hard to read, but when I looked at the beginning there was my name at the root of the major vein. It was the beginning. I was the beginning. Three lines were travelling from mine. The first intersected a lot of other words and numbers on the page, but stopped before the page had even ended.

My eyes travelled back to the middle line, and I followed a few words like birth, and choice and *Sealatia* until it had Merrick's name written. This line intersected so many of the other lines on the rest of the page, spreading out the longest length and swirling here and there until there was no space left on the page. It disappeared before I could see where it ended. There were too many words for me to read or make out clearly. Some of them written over top of each other, scrambling their true meaning.

The final line emerged from the root beneath the bone into the same first few words as the middle line had, words like birth, and *Sealatia*. Only, it separated from where Merrick's name had been written. Instead, it had Zale's name etched into the surface. This line ended way before the others. The word death inscribed on the page before it travelled very much further. I should have been relieved that it had provided me some answers. I was meant to be with Merrick. Or so this reading seemed to suggest. Yet, the bone reading hadn't truly answered my biggest question of all.

As I looked at the page again I tried to read some of the words intersecting the middle line, but they were all quite tangled in a mess. Frustrated, I let out a deep sigh. I still wasn't so sure what it meant, but at least I knew why Zale had asked Merrick to choose me. It seemed like I might have the best life with him.

Chapter 19

I HAD BEEN SPENDING more and more time with my Dad on the weekends helping him organize all the analysis data printouts that he needed for work. Since organization was apparently my forte, he had been asking me to help him pretty steadily.

School seemed to be slacking and I finished my assignments shortly after I got them, but Leah and Evie were increasingly busy with all their studying and we hung out after classes less and less. We were all anxious for summer vacation to arrive.

Today, as usual, I had travelled with my dad down to the Science buildings where he and my mother worked. It was a Saturday, but he was always putting in overtime so it was to be expected. He was busy typing away at his computer when he looked up at me taking a pause.

"So Anya, there's been a verdict on that summer opportunity at the Cap Pele base camp that I wanted to discuss with you."

I prayed it had nothing to do with the *Sealatians*, on my behalf he had submitted an application for me to participate.

"What is it Dad?" I asked eagerly, but I feared his answer.

"Well your mother and I have been accepted as two of the chairs on the summer research program in Cap Pele this year."

"On the beach program there."

"Yes, and I found out today that the student position available has been offered to you as well. It would be something like an internship where you would have the chance to assist us with some of the fieldwork."

"Oh," I said, "so we're going and you want me to accept and come with you? I don't see what else I would be doing this summer." I had never really spent much time away from my parents.

"Well that's the thing, Caspian and Ondine offered for you to stay with them this summer if you like. That way you're not too far away from your friends, and Merrick, of course."

"Really?"

"Yep, you bet. We just want to make sure that you're happy over your summer vacation."

"I'll have to think about it," I said. My father looked surprised. I think he had expected me to want to stay behind.

"You know, Anya, you can invite Merrick over more often if you like. You don't have to worry about your mother and I thinking it strange for you to be alone with him. Your mother tells me you worry too much."

"I...I... she said that?" The conversation had taken an unexpected turn and now I was starting to worry that my parents would begin asking for Merrick to come over more often.

"You're a good Mer, Anya. Your mother and I trust that you won't do anything you're not ready for, and well we know you are responsible. Otherwise we wouldn't feel comfortable leaving you on your own."

"Thanks Dad."

"It's just that sometimes we think you're too hard on yourself and maybe limiting yourself too much. You might be a quarter human, but we don't follow the same practices as them. Heck you're going to marry Merrick; you should be taking some time to get to know him better, and him you. I've seen the way he looks at you."

Those words had me utterly appalled. "What do you mean the way he looks at me? Dad!"

"Tiger Shark, you know he's going to have to love you, you're too wonderful for him not to."

"Oh Dad!"

"I can see it though, he definitely cares for you."

"Ummhmm," I said not really wanting to discuss Merrick with my father anymore. "I should go outside and check on the samples." It was the perfect excuse to slip away from him since it actually needed to be done quite often.

I slipped into my lab coat and put on my gloves and protective glasses. It's not like the water samples were toxic or acidic or could harm me, but there were qualities found in them that linked to our underwater cities. Particles or plant life were indicative of our sophistication and needed to always be kept a secret. For that reason when going into the samples building set up like an outdoor tent it was always necessary to wear required gear.

The science Mers were a little paranoid if you asked me, but I understood that this was how things were done and so I didn't complain. What I found funnier was the lack of security or security equipment on site. The employees did have pass cards for entrance at the main gate and for the main building, but the rest of the buildings were not so easily controlled or regulated.

As I rounded the corner on the building my father and I had been in, I spotted a few of my father's co-workers with Arturo up ahead and walking towards me. He was directing them to follow him though they seemed to be in protest.

"Arturo, we left piles of printouts back there, we can't just leave them and move onto the next site with you." The taller of the two Mers was wearing a similar get up to mine and I had to admit it was quite comical.

"My assistant will deal with those," he said firmly in his no nonsense tone, and pulled out a walkie talkie pressing the button that he dialled to connect with the other side. The static on the other line was abysmal, but he barked orders into it that the papers should be gathered from Site 3, and then nodded to the other scientists. They seemed satisfied with that, and I waved at him while I passed. He smiled at me and then returned his sharp gaze back to the other Mers. I sure was glad that I was not either of them right now. Arturo may have been like an uncle to me, but I knew that he was an incredibly powerful Mer in the science world, and I would hate to ever get on his bad side.

Walking around the corner of another building the glint of sun in the distance caught my eyes and distracted me from looking forward. I collided seconds later with another body. Only I realized afterwards that I had been the only one moving. I bent to grab my protective lenses which had fallen in the scramble and grew embarrassed. "I'm so sorry," I began, "I wasn't paying attention and the sun distracted me and..."

"It's alright, Anya," the other voice said and I recognized it immediately. When I looked back at the person, there they were, those haunting teal eyes that I could picture with my eyes closed.

"Merrick what are you doing here?" I asked surprised to see him at the Science base camp.

"I came to see you," he said flashing a charming smile. I could feel slight hesitation in his words and knew something was not right.

"Why are you lying to me?" I asked, afraid I wouldn't like the answer. He shouldn't be there, how had he even been given access to the base camp for Science Mers. I knew he could do anything he wanted at the soldier outpost, but here was a completely different story.

His face fell. He grew serious. "You think I'm lying?"

"Aren't you?" I asked with my eyebrow raised.

"No." He began, "Anya, I thought you agreed you wouldn't use that power on me."

"I'm sorry," I said, "I didn't. It's just that a feeling glimmered out of you and it made me wonder." I grew embarrassed. I wasn't often wrong with my emotional reads.

"It's okay," he said touching my elbow lightly, "you can make it up to me with a tour."

"A tour?" I said. "Wouldn't you just find that boring?"

"What makes you say that Anya? Is it because I'm a warrior Mer? Meant to be a strong and captivating soldier? I'm a brute force, not a brain." He was teasing me.

"Yes of course Merrick. Your attention span couldn't take the calculations and explanations of how we measure water with graduated cylinders."

He stopped and looked down at me. "My, aren't we saucy."

I wiggled my nose at him and he bent down and kissed it; I hadn't expected him to be so affectionate and was surprised, excited by how close he was to me. He straightened, looking a little embarrassed so I hugged him to show him how happy I was with his presence and affection. He hugged me back just as lovingly and I could have swooned. It was moments like this that made me wonder why I had ever doubted him before, but then he had never managed to voice to me what he felt.

"Well what are you doing here anyway?"

"One of my dad's friends is attending a meeting regarding the use of some scientific research to support our warriors out in the field against the Depths. So I am here tagging along to find out more about our interactions between the two groups. I guess you could say it's like an internship."

"Oh" I said surprised that he had been doing a similar career development type thing with the warrior Mers. The Depths were dangerous creatures that lurked in the coldest parts of the ocean. Inky and shadow-like they came out every few years to decimate coral populations and in more recent years had even gone as far as attacking a Mer city. The Mers had formed a research league to find out more about the mysterious creature.

"Yeah, but he found out that you were here today too. So he insisted that after the meeting I take some time to track my betrothed down while he finished up with some of the so-called boring standard stuff. Apparently, I already know how to handle those things."

"I didn't know you were in a Mer internship Merrick, you never told me that."

"I don't like to brag," he said jokingly. Sometimes he was so charming I wanted to grab him and kiss the senses out of him. I bit my lip as punishment for my thoughts and his eyes immediately followed the movement. He smiled wickedly and looked around before pushing me back against the outer wall of the building.

"I must say Anya, you're looking awfully cute with those glasses on. Maybe we should skip the tour and make out instead."

"Merrick," I said disapprovingly. The last thing I needed was for my dad to come searching for me and stumble upon me necking.

"Fine," he said tucking my hair behind my ear. "Torment me."

I rolled my eyes at him. "Come on," I said, "I have to go measure some samples and take some readings."

"Lead the way," he said as I grabbed his hand, our fingers interlocking. It was the first time we had held hands, and as seemingly juvenile the gesture, it made me want to blush with delight. His fingers interlaced with mine.

We reached the way station and he was patiently watching me measure things.

"I can picture you working here all summer, except with a little bucket hat on your head and some sandals." I laughed at the image.

"You sure have an imagination, mister." I hesitated before I spoke. I hadn't really told anyone that I had planned to take my dad up on his offer. "but, I don't think that I'm going to be here this summer Merrick."

"I knew that."

"How?" I wondered if my father had mentioned anything to him.

"Zale," he said. He seemed colder suddenly, more distant. I wondered if what had happened in the dream still bothered him, but I did not want to mention it to rub salt in the wound.

"Oh. Well, I was thinking that the summer internship in Cap Pele my parents mentioned to me would be an excellent opportunity, so I might take it."

I suddenly wondered just how much Zale had told him about me. *How many choices had Zale witnessed in my life and why?*

"Well have fun in Cap Pele then." He seemed so nonchalant to the point where I wondered if it bothered him.

"Your parents offered for me to stay with your family."

"I know."

"Well would you want that?"

"It doesn't matter what I want." I wondered what he meant by that, and why he seemed so controlled. I wanted to send out my feelers to sense his emotions, but I had promised him that I wouldn't.

"Okay," I replied still unsure about his response. I guess I wanted more out of him, some inclination that he might want me around.

"Anya, you should do what you want." Well I guess that was my answer.

"I will." I said finishing with the last measurement and marking it into the computer with a few keystrokes.

"So what is all of this information you have here?" He asked lifting the edge of the reports printed out next to the computer.

"Just the water analysis report."

"Do you always keep such excessive copies of these things?

"I guess so. Since I started here, it seems to be

the way that they do things."

"Well, can you print another report?" He asked me and I was starting to wonder what he was getting at.

"You want to take one of the reports?" I asked pushing my protective lenses back on the bridge of my nose.

"Well just so I can keep it for the Sergeant I'm helping."

"What would he need a water analysis report for?"

"Well they were discussing the water information near the spawning point for the Depths and this could be good comparative data."

I wasn't completely convinced with his explanation, but Merrick had never lied to me. He never gave me any cause to suspect him of something sinister.

"Yeah I can print another one Merrick, but you know that this has to stay within the Mer community."

"I know," he said. "I would never jeopardize the work the science Mers do.

"Here," I said handing the stack to him and then, keying in another printout. We waited a few minutes for everything to print and I gathered it and stapled it together.

"Well I'm all done here. Did you want to come back with me to the lab? My dad would probably like to say hi."

"I'd like to," he began, "but I should get back to that meeting. I know the Sergeant will want my notes on the Depths and I hid them on him."

He walked over to me a little stilted before leaning down and kissing my cheek. It felt so formal and unlike the Merrick who had been flirting with me not even ten minutes before.

"Thanks Anya."

"You're welcome Merrick." I said watching him turn around and leave. Then I had a thought. *Had Merrick only wanted the printout of the information?* Was that why there was the glimmer of deceit from him when he had first spotted me? It didn't matter though, apparently I was going to keep giving him what he wanted.

Chapter 20

MY WEEK OFF FOR MARCH break seemed to pass and before I knew it, once again I found myself seated in an English class next to Seth and Evie and listening to Mr. Little speak rapidly about literary tropes.

Class let out, and Seth walked Evie and me to my locker. Lately, he had been hanging out with us after classes more and I suspected it was because he had a crush on one of my friends. The thing was that I couldn't really tell who. He'd become quite the flirt.

"Seth and I are going to go get some chocolate milk before next period Anya, you want some?" Evie asked.

"No, but thanks though", I said

"Only for you," Seth added with a wink before he turned and walked with Evie in the direction of the cafeteria. I turned back to my locker and pulled out my art portfolio. This class was going to be a free period, so I wanted to make use of the time I had to get our final project finished.

"Hey Anya," His voice brushed against my ears in such a pleasing tone, but I was still annoyed with him for using me for information.

"What do you want Merrick?" I said turning to him my neck having to crane up higher than I had anticipated. We hadn't seen each other at all during March break. The one time that we had made tentative plans, he had bailed on me. Seeing him I was caught off guard, he looked even better now than he had the last time. He was taller and filled out more, while my only big change was my shoulder length hair and five pounds in weight. His eyes brightened at my surprise.

"You're even taller!" I said, not hiding my disdain.

The corner of his mouth pulled up into a smile. "You'll have to play catch up pipsqueak."

My eyes immediately narrowed, and I squared my shoulders placing my hands on my hips.

"Seriously Merrick!" He flicked my nose, and I grabbed his hand annoyed pinching the skin between his fingers as hard as I could.

"Ouch," he said shaking his hand before leaning against the lockers behind me. I felt as though his looming height was casting a shadow over my body. "Come on Anya, be nice to me." He pleaded.

I rolled my eyes. "I am always nice to you."

He looked at me, and then twisted his mouth, "You are, but you could be nicer." I always felt gutted when he started to get flirtatious.

"What do you want?" I repeated.

"Who says I want anything?" He asked.

"That look on your face tells me," I said. "Plus you don't exactly stop by to say 'hello', now do you?"

He looked a little sad before he spoke. "Am I always like that?"

"It's not a big deal Merrick. So...?"

"Well, could you maybe get me more printouts of that water and fish scale analysis report?"

"What? No!" I said answering quickly. "What do you even need that for? And don't tell me a science project. I know you don't take chemistry."

"How do you know I don't take chemistry?"

"Oh didn't you know? I follow the Merrick Price fan page online, that those cute cheerleaders set up." I pretended to shake pom poms and he snorted, running a hand through his hair.

"I have an environmental science thing I'm volunteering for and I think the research would help." I turned and looked at him suspiciously. Pearl had mentioned something about a Wetlands field trip she was going on that she thought I should attend. Maybe they were related.

"The information is for Mers only Merrick."

"Of course Anya, I'm going to be the only one looking at it, I swear."

Just then, Gina and her friend appeared at the end of the hallway and were making their way in our direction. Merrick followed my eyes and glanced at them before licking his lips almost nervously. "Please babe?"

Babe? My mind raced, it was the first time he had ever called me by a term of endearment and it was reckless with Gina so close by. I couldn't lie to myself and pretend that it hadn't affected me. I actually kind of liked it, and nodded soundlessly before tilting my head towards Gina and speaking with my eyes that he should go.

"You're the best." He said before walking up behind Gina and her friend and joining their conversation.

Ugh! I wanted to wring my hands. Why couldn't

I say no to him? *Because he's your betrothed dummy*! I yelled at myself mentally.

I HAD FORGOTTEN MY ART book in my locker. How I had managed to do that I wasn't sure, maybe it had to do with my complete lack of coordination that week. I was feeling lonely lately and I didn't know what would have brought such a feeling on. I had been spending a lot of time with my friends so the feeling felt absurd, unnecessary.

Walking down the hallway, I could hear voices speaking intimately. I prayed I wasn't going to stumble upon a couple necking. That would only leave me more reeling. The past couple of weeks had flown by and I felt as though time was speeding ahead dangerously, like if I closed my eyes for too long I would wake up and it would be the summer. At least the weather was improving, but something just didn't sit well with me over March Break. It had been quiet, haunting almost.

"What do you mean, Jericho?" I heard the voice say with a giggle. That voice was familiar, grating, and a shiver crawled up my spine.

"Come, on," he replied, "forget about that other guy, you know it's me you want. Don't you remember how much fun we had together last weekend? Don't you remember what I did for you?"

I rounded the corner faster, my heart pounding, could it really be who I thought it was. That damn voice that was like nails on a chalkboard every time that pouty mouth opened.

It was Gina!

He was leaning in for a kiss, and her eyes opened wide when she saw me and she swatted him away quickly.

"Jerry, please! I don't know what you're talking

about."

His eyes followed hers to me. Jericho Maitson, captain of the basketball and football teams. He was a senior, graduating this year with a scholarship to a school somewhere out west.

I didn't stare, I knew better, instead, carefully, slowly I moved towards my locker and opened it, thank goodness Evie had put a mirror up in there. I pretended to put on my lip gloss and then rummage for my art book. I heard the heaviest sign escape from what could only be a male.

"G, I'm getting sick of these secrets," he said trying to be low enough so that I would not hear. "I'll see you after school," he said and let out another huge sigh before I heard the shuffle of his clothing as he left.

Had it been anyone else I would have been embarrassed for stumbling upon them. Instead I was intrigued. *Did she know that Merrick had kissed me?* I supposed that he and I weren't any better. Then again, I had no idea what Gina and Merrick's arrangement involved. I only knew that Merrick was going to be my husband.

"Anna?" I heard behind me.

"Uhhh," that made it worse. I turned around really slowly.

"Look that wasn't what you thought at all," she said to me her chin tilted high.

"Oh?" I ask, "mind reader, are you? So what was I thinking G-Dog?" I wasn't impressed with her attitude. I looked her straight in the eye.

She seemed to weaken for a moment before she caught herself and shook it off. "Whatever, look Jericho is just a family friend, so it's not really any of your business what we were talking about."

She was right about that, it wasn't any of my

business, and it was sure as shell something that I did not want to know more about. The only thing on my mind at that moment, was Merrick. *Did he know Gina was hanging out with Jericho Maitson in empty hallways during class time? Would it hurt him? Should I tell him?*

"Look, just forget whatever you saw here, or you'll be sorry." Gina looked down her nose at me. She was threatening me, and yet all I could feel was amusement. "No one would believe you anyway." She turned on her heel and started to walk away.

"You're right Gina," I said, stopping her from going further. I couldn't stop myself, the words came spilling out before I could reel them back in. She glanced back at me puzzled.

"No one would ever believe that Jericho Maitland was interested in you."

I don't know why I did it, but I did. In that one cruel moment, I had stooped to her level and attacked her self-esteem. I thought she was going to attack me, like a vicious dog attacking its prey. Her face twisted into the starting of her pounce, but we were interrupted.

"Ladies, are we having a social meeting in the hallway?" It was Mrs. Humpries, the school guidance counsellor.

"No, Mrs. Humpries, we are not," I answered calmly. "I came to get my art book." and then flashed her my hall pass. I had baited her, yes, but Gina always seemed to have a case of the crazies around me. It didn't take much to bring her from zero to one hundred on the anger scale with me.

"Ummm I was just headed to class Mrs. H," Gina said swallowing nervously.

I didn't want to stick around to witness. Mrs Humpries was a stickler, and hated it when students called her Mrs. H, I knew that Gina was going to get detention. There was no need for me to watch her awkward moment. I had a feeling that if I took any longer, anyway, my art teacher would start to get concerned.

Chapter 21

By the end of the month, I was ready to give Merrick the research that he needed. I had managed to get it the following day, but I wanted to be able to talk to him alone. I didn't feel comfortable just handing it to him in the hallway with Gina and a bunch of his male Mer friends around. I also didn't want Pearl to know what I had done. Even though there was nothing bad about my actions, it felt like it should remain secretive between Merrick and I, so I couldn't give it to her to give to him. Since Rayne had finished high school a semester early, Pearl and I spent a lot more time in the library together now, and both of us saw Merrick during school less and less.

I took a deep breath and walked down the hall near the entrance where Merrick's locker was and where I knew he would be at the beginning of his lunch break. I wasn't lucky enough to catch him alone. He was surrounded by his and Gina's friends. I approached them slowly.

"Oh watch out Merrick, whale incoming!" Murdock teased turning his attention to me. "Hey Anya, did you eat any krill today?" He added making weird snacking noises.

    I shook my head in disgust. Since I was still quite small, Murdock had taken to making fun of my weight by calling me a whale. How his metaphor worked- I didn't know, but the other Mers in his crew seemed to find it funny regardless. I couldn't wait to fill out properly. I had only gained ten pounds since my scaling and that wasn't enough to show much on me- at all. Mermaids are supposed to be well insulated, we swim in the coldest depths of the ocean, but I was tired of feeling bad for something I couldn't control. Now that I had transcended, it would only be a matter of time before I looked like a true mermaid. I was so irritated by the time I stopped in front of Merrick's turned back, that I didn't care that Gina and her friends were standing there, I shot an insult back to Murdock in *Mecrutian*. I knew I probably shouldn't have lowered myself to his level, but my temper got the best of me.

    Some of his friends snickered, and through his laughing at Murdock, Havelock managed to say, "Ooooo burn!"

    "What did she just say?" Gina asked and Murdock's eyes darkened.

    "It doesn't matter," he said wiping his nose as though he were completely offended.

    "You asked for that," Merrick said.

    "Look, Merrick," I said trying to control my voice, "can I talk to you for a sec? I have that info you needed."

    "No, you may not talk to my boyfriend," Gina said. "We have lunch plans, skeletor." She crossed her arms and stepped in front of Merrick.

Everything that she said stung. Boyfriend. Skeletor. My jaw ticked and I knew my eyes went dark. I licked my lips annoyed with her presence. I would have liked to throw some magic on her, but I would never live it down in the Mer community. Plus, I had to be the bigger person. I had been so far, why would I change.

"Whatever, enjoy your lunch, G-Dog."

I saluted her and moved on. As I walked away I could hear Merrick speak loudly. "Why do you have to be that way Gina? She was doing me a favour."

I had made it halfway down the hall when a strong arm was pulling me around. Merrick brushed his hair out of his face.

"I'm sorry about that babe, you didn't deserve that." His eyes were soft. I was still frowning, but when Merrick called me babe it was like every bad feeling went away and I melted a little on the inside.

"Wanna turn that frown upside down?" He asked with his usual charm.

I pulled out the papers from my book bag and swatted him in the shoulder with them before I handed them over. He was looking at them carefully, and nodded his head in approval.

Before I could stop myself the question blurted out of my mouth. "Do you call Gina babe too?" I tucked a stray hair behind my ear, but it fell forward again in rebellion.

"No," he said looking up from the papers. "I call Gina, Gina."

"Why not sweetie, or cupcake, or love muffin?" I asked wanting to know what exactly she was to him. I had experienced firsthand part of what he felt for her when we had been skating, but he was different with the both of us.

"Love muffin?" he questioned before he

continued, "those would all suggest she's sweet."

"Yeah," I said, "they're terms of endearment."

His eyes had a sparkle as he spoke. "Well she's not exactly sweet, now is she?" He spoke again before I could, wiggling the papers. "Listen, thanks for these."

"Wait," I said, trying to stop him before he returned to them.

Over March break I had taken the time to carve a shell pendant with Merrick's name on it in *Mecrutian*. I had planned to give it to him early on the platonic date we had scheduled that never came to fruition. His birthday was the last day of the month and even though that was a few days away, I had a feeling I probably wouldn't see him again for some time. I had hung it on a black leather cord to set off the iridescent blues in the white of the surface. He watched me closely as I lifted the necklace from my beneath sweater and pulled it over my head.

"Happy early Birthday Merrick," I said holding my hand out to him with the wrapped up necklace hidden beneath my fingers. Gina had kept glancing over at us, but she had been distracted long enough with one of her friends while I had taken it off, to miss me placing it into my palm.

"I made it, so don't throw it out," I said wondering if he would ever wear it. He reached out and took it delicately from my hand.

"Thank you Anya," he said sliding it into his pocket. Then he turned around and headed back to his crew. I watched him walk away, I didn't care if Gina saw me and when he glanced back at me there was surprise in his eyes that I had been so bold. I was no longer annoyed or angry so I gave him a slow and sassy smile as best I could. Gina could chew on that during their lunch, and I didn't really care, not even if it landed Merrick in hot water with her.

For a moment, I thought he might frown or give me a dirty look for being so reckless, but instead he just stared at me, that same look that made my insides melt until Gina grabbed his arm and pulled him out the door.

MERRICK KEPT HIS DISTANCE for the entire months of April and May. The few times we had spoken had been in the school hallways and our conversations hadn't been about much of anything. Idle chit chat about the weather or his sisters. Part of me regretted ever giving him that stupid necklace. Pearl had said that I shouldn't take it personally. He was busy with driving lessons, and shopping for a motorcycle or a car so that was taking up most of his time. Not to mention the fact that Gina was as demanding as ever.

I dreamed of him, often. It was the same dream continuing over and over again. I was on the beach, him in the water, bathed in moonlight and me never quite reaching him. The tide always pulled him away from me, the closer I tried to get. Finally though, in my most recent dream, I had reached him and he had embraced me, and it was then I realized that his tail was far paler than the colour I had expected. It was silver and glinting off the rays of moon beams. He had wrapped his arms around me ,and we sank down beneath the surface, his mouth kissing mine as we fell into the blackness below. Deeper and deeper, we drifted down, until I could see only the faint outline of him before me, and the only warmth I felt was from his touch. I could faintly see his hair float up and wisp out, and then all of a sudden, a light pierced through the darkness. It was coming from his chest and when it dimmed slightly, relieving the ache in my eyes I realized it was from the heart of shell I had carved for him. It had melded with his flesh. We slowly floated back up to the surface, and as the water slid off of us there were voices, threatening and angry, calling to us from the shore. When I turned to see them, I awoke.

    The dream had haunted me for days and it was like Merrick somehow knew that I was thinking of him because I didn't see him that week, not even once at school in the hallways. I scolded myself every time my eyes searched for him, but I couldn't help it, I had felt such peace and joy with him in the dream, in his arms that I wanted to see him, even if it was just for one moment. School kept on though, and I charged my way through it, distracting myself by putting all my efforts into my work. I was the one planning to leave soon for the summer, but I still couldn't help, but feel like I was the one rejected.

    IT WAS A BEAUTIFUL SUMMER day in the last week of school, but neither of us, Pearl or me, had felt much like basking in the sun. So we had both retreated to the school library where we hid in the stacks and pulled out interesting Art History books and Photography compilations. My mood seemed to match Pearl's.

    Even though Merlin and her would spend most of the summer together, he had found out that his training was extending an extra two weeks because of some storms in the South Pacific. There was an attack on a Mer village by the Depths. His instructors had been recruited to help in the fight, and so all of the students in his training class had to wait for their dismissal.

    She felt as though she should be excited that she would see him soon, but the extra few weeks of waiting were hard on her already saddened Mer soul.

Rayne had left early, planned to finish her schooling so that she could be with her mate. It was harder for them to be apart. Even Coral and Murdock had grown closer, and he had taken her out on a few dates lately with the hopes that the two of them could at least become amicable. It seemed as though things were better between them, and at least Coral distracted him from annoying me. I wondered why Merrick and I didn't feel the same draw to one another, though at moments like this I knew that we'd been apart for too long. I craved seeing him, worse than a chocolate craving and nothing seemed to help.

"How can you spend the whole summer away?" Pearl asked me for the fifth time that day. Only this time I didn't elaborate on what an excellent opportunity it was to get the placement, or the fact that the beach in Cap Pele was gorgeous, or that I had plans to explore as much of New Brunswick as I could on my weekends off, instead I simply answered what my mood made me feel. "I don't know."

"You'll come back," she said with a happier tone, noticing my tinge of sadness.

"I will." I said.

"Thank goodness," she said with a smile, she leaned her head towards me and I tilted mine so that we were braced against each other affectionately.

"I'm going to miss him," I admitted, "a lot."

"He'll miss you too." She said and almost had me convinced.

"No, he'll have Gina," I said. "He'll be fine."

"She's not the same as you Anya. She can't compare."

I nodded and puffed out a breath, but honestly I wasn't convinced.

Chapter 22

I WAS LEAVING FOR Cap Pele. Everything was packed and ready to go. My parents had loaded up the car, and we were just checking over the last few rooms in the house when the telephone rang. I prayed it was Merrick, my last visit with Coral and Pearl before I left he was noticeably absent and they had not commented much on where he was.

"I'll get it!" I shouted, excited to be going away for a few months, maybe it would clear my head, get me away from my dreams of him, and Gina's incessant dirty looks. I needed some time for myself. I wanted to figure out more of what I wanted.

"Hello, may I please speak with Anya?"

"Speaking," I answered. "Merrick?" I asked, even though it did not sound like him.

"Uhhh, it's Seth. I got your number from Leah and Evie. Were you expecting a call from someone else? I can let you go."

"Oh, hey Seth, no no, it's fine" I said, "sorry

about that. What's up?"

"I well, Evie and Leah told me you were going away for the summer so I just wanted to say bye."

"Oh, thanks, that's nice of you. I'll be back," I said in a *Terminator* voice.

He laughed. "Yeah, I can't wait. I just, I wanted to wish you a good summer vacation was all."

"You too, Seth, make sure that Leah and Evie don't miss me too much," I joked.

"Yeah, I'll try," he started, "But you're pretty hard to replace." My stomach did a back flip, I missed Merrick sneaking in nice things like that. It made me me feel stronger than I thought and for a moment I felt that had I been normal, had things been different, I might have forgotten all about Merrick and paid more attention to Seth.

"Anya!" My mom called to me from the front door.

"Be right there!" I said shifting the phone to the side so as not to pop Seth's eardrum.

"Well you gotta go," he said.

"Yeah, sorry!"

"Listen, uh don't forget me Anya."

I smiled, suddenly realizing that I was the one Seth liked in our group. How I missed that I wasn't so sure.

"Of course I won't. Bye Seth!"

I hung up the phone and ran down the stairs to meet my parents at the car.

"Who was that my mom asked?"

"Merrick?" My father guessed hopefully.

"Oh, no it was Seth," a friend from school.

"A boy?" My mother asked with disapproval.

"A friend. Don't worry so much. Mom, can we get this show on the road?" I slid on her extra pair of sunglasses, and she smiled.

"Those look nice on you, sweetheart."

With the car pulling out of the driveway, I wondered if this summer would be as full of change as the past ten months. Deep down, I almost wished for some quiet, but I knew that wouldn't happen, I had only begun my transcendence.

"Oh this letter came for you," my mom said handing me the envelope with a smiley scribbled on the front of it.

I held my breath opening the manila envelope and hoped that it was from Merrick. It was from Zale.

Anya,

I know you're disappointed, you were probably hoping that idiot brother of mine had taken the time to write you a little note before you left. You won't understand now, but it's probably for the better that he didn't write to you. He and I are in Peggy's Cove today so we won't be able to see you off, as much as I might like to give you another peck.

A winking smiley face was scribbled in the margin with a slightly crooked smile and I wanted to laugh at it, but then I remembered how upset Merrick had been when he'd heard about the dream. That had to mean something, he had even said "he knows you're my mate." That meant I was part of his life, even if lately he had made it habit to ignore me. For a moment, I thought that perhaps I should discount Zale's confession, but I returned to my reading.

Merrick would have a fit though, and I'm not one to take enjoyment from my brother's pain. All the same, when you get back, you and I will have much to discuss. Enjoy your summer, and don't forget about us. Be patient with him Anya, he means

well.
 I'll miss your lovely smile.

I smiled, and folded the letter placing it back in the envelope. Again, Zale had surprised me, and I wondered what we would need to discuss when I returned, clearly it would have to do with Merrick.
I let my feelings melt off of me. There was no point in letting all of these mystery emotions take over the enjoyment of my trip with my parents. In this moment something exciting was happening in my life. I rolled down the window to let the rays of sun shine stroke my face and let the song on the radio invade my senses.
No matter what happened over the summer there was one thing I finally knew, regardless of how Merrick felt, or how much I realized that I cared about him, we would have time on our side to make things work. Our hearts couldn't be broken so easily, they weren't made of shell.

About the Author

Zara Steen has a penchant for paranormal and fantasy romance. She lives in Atlantic Canada with her partner and is always thinking of new book ideas and characters. Her second installment of The Mercrutian Chronicles: Blue Moon Rising is anticipated to be released in 2016.

Check out her forthcoming books Young Adult Books at: www.zarasteen.com.

Made in the USA
Charleston, SC
30 November 2015